UNEXPECTED

SERENDIPITY

THE SOREN FAMILY

NICOLE VIDAL

COPYRIGHT

Cover design by Ashlee Nassar of Designs with Sass

Cover photos by Kiefer Photography/Shutterstock

Developmental Edit by Rob Martin of Hot Tree Editing

Final Edit by Sharron McKenzie of Hot Tree Editing

ISBN 978-1-961365-71-1

TABLE OF CONTENTS

KEEP IN TOUCH WITH NV

Facebook (http://fb.me/NicoleVidalAuthor)

Instagram (http://instagram.com/nicolevidal_author)

Amazon (https://www.amazon.com/Nicole-Vidal/e/B082DJHPXP?ref_=dbs_p_ebk_r00_abau_000000)

My website (www.nicolevidal.com)

Pinterest (http://pinterest.com/NicoleVidal_Author)

Goodreads (https://www.goodreads.com/author/show/19827329.Nicole_Vidal)

CHAPTER ONE

SERAPHINA

It was a beautiful ceremony. My brother Lexington Soren, heir to a billion-dollar shipping company, married for love. It's true Lex and Keeley agreed to a marriage of convenience, but they quickly realized they were meant to be. I'm grateful the same restrictions weren't placed on me by my late father. I'm single, childless, underemployed, and rich as hell. The kicker is most people assume I'm barely getting by because I don't flaunt my wealth. I have my vices, but most people don't see them.

"Where are you heading now, Elle?" I ask my oldest sister while we wait for our vehicles at the valet stand of the wedding venue.

"Home. You?"

"Same. Aren't Cora and Wes going to their dad's?"

"Yeah, why?" Ellery and her husband are embroiled in a nasty divorce. Like Lex, she was forced to marry an appropriately stationed man. My sister demanded fidelity. Her almost-ex didn't follow through and violated their prenuptial agreement. Unfortunately for my soon-to-be former brother-in-law, Elle's wealth is up in the air. Lex's attorney is looking into the intricate details and what we are entitled to, given our parentage. It's messy to say the least.

"Just checking in. No big deal. I'll see you at brunch when Lex and Keeley return from their honeymoon. Love you."

"See you then," my oldest sister answers.

"You sure you're okay?"

Her tone isn't sitting well with me. Ellery is as intelligent as she is beautiful. She's tall, thin, and blonde. I would kill for her hair. In hindsight, with knowledge of our parents' affairs, we look nothing alike. While I am tall, my hair is chestnut, and my eyes are hazel like my brother.

"I'm happy Lex married the right one the first time." She shrugs. "I'm angry I didn't stand up for myself."

"You wouldn't have Cora and Wes, if you did." Weston is twelve, and his leukemia is in remission. His sister is ten, and she's a certified genius. So much so that she's taking classes two years ahead.

"They are the only bright spots of my marriage to—" She looks left then right. "—the lying, cheating sleaze."

I politely stifle a laugh, and Elle smiles. Worth it. Our cars arrive, and we hug briefly and go our separate ways.

My parents, Baldwin and Cecile née Westwood, had five children—one son and four daughters. Much like they expected of my brother, my parents weren't soulmates. Their marriage looked good on paper. I'm not even sure they were ever friends.

Soon before Lex's wedding, we learned that neither of my parents were faithful. After lashing out at Lex because he's in charge now, my sisters and I submitted to DNA testing. Only two of us are offspring of Baldwin and Cecile. Me and Lex. The fact that my sisters are not full siblings led to turmoil with our family trust. Based on his estate plan, it seems my father was aware Ellery and Sky were not his daughters sooner than the rest of us. The truth is, Dad likely knew after Ellery's arranged marriage but before Sky's. My younger sister's husband wasn't selected for her or on an acceptable list. Like Lex, she married for love. Unfortunately, she was widowed a few years later.

Old money is an apt description for the Soren family. Celt Industries is a multi-national shipping company. It was formed by my grandfather, Sumner. He built it from the ground up. While doing so, he managed to exemplify what a stable marriage looks like.

Sumner and Collette had an epic love story. They met in high school and stayed together while my grandfather honorably served our country. Their letters are romantic and poignant. Nana was keen to share their contents, minus the spicy bits, before her death. Their bond was what classic romances are made of. Aside from their mutual love of movies and each other, they were truly friends. Their friendship carried them through many tough times, including the tragic loss of two children at once and a hostile takeover attempt of Celt Industries. Thinking about my grandparents pushes my thoughts back to the present issues.

I'll gain access to my trust fund without any outside control when I turn thirty. The terms of my trust are simple. Tuition and living expenses were to be paid through college and graduate education, if applicable. Once I finished school, I received monthly living expenses as long as I'm employed. Soon, I'll be granted complete control of the funds with a degree and a job. I would be bored to tears if I didn't work. There are only so many material things a girl could buy. There are no other stipulations. It's laughable that employment is required, considering the value of my trust is north of five billion dollars. Until recently, the five of us were treated equally. Now, I could end up with half of the family fortune. The possibility of having that much money is a foreign concept to me. It will take some getting used to. My family has set up generational wealth. More importantly, my grandfather is alive, meaning additional funds will be added to the corpus when he dies. My family is filthy rich. I suppose I am as well. The difference is, I don't share that fact with anyone. More importantly, no one expects a bookstore manager could be an Ivy-League educated heiress.

Instead of returning to my loft, I park near the center of Mystic Cove. The town is quaint and picturesque. There are a few distinct areas. Downtown is a busy street lined with restaurants, boutiques, Seaside Books, and Coffee & Confections. It's one location of Keeley's bakery business. My sister-in-law is a magician with pastry dough. There's a working drawbridge and a small park along the waterfront.

I exit my car and take a seat on one of the wooden benches. It's near ten in the evening, but happy couples mill around. Ever since my siblings and I learned that our parents' vows were simply suggestions, I was glad to be single. Now, after watching my brother find his person and meet the requirements of the Celt board, I may be rethinking my position.

As a small boat passes by with a couple dancing on deck despite the chilly air, I resolve to be open to the possibility of finding love again. I dated in high school… sort of. My mother was a hawk. She scrutinized the boys who dared ask me to homecoming or the prom. Each one was properly and thoroughly vetted based on their bloodline and place on the wealthiest families list. By the time I was a senior at my fancy boarding school, I simply attended solo. Alone was easier.

At UPenn, I had a steady and mother-approved boyfriend. Pierce Thornton Wallace was premed. We were quite compatible. My relationship with Pierce lasted until halfway through our senior year. Despite his family's money and tutoring, he underperformed in his classes. On top of that, he didn't score well on the MCAT, which is the admission test for medical school. Once my mother heard he was failing and had no future in her terms, our parents forbade us to see each other anymore. We tried to keep our relationship under the radar, but it was futile. When you're as wealthy as my family, eyes and ears are everywhere.

Content my future husband won't serendipitously appear, I wander back to my car and return home. Perhaps someday my someone will appear. It's truly the only thing missing in my life. That, and a seat on the board.

CHAPTER TWO

SERAPHINA

Two weeks have flown by. I hurry to my car and drive to my brother's home. I understand his desire to keep people out, but the gate is a bit much for me.

I park in front of the modern home with stunning views of the Atlantic Ocean and climb the staircase. As I'm about to ring the bell, the door swings open. Keeley is beautiful in a fitted red dress. It's perfect for her curvy figure.

"Look at you. You're tan and appear thoroughly rested. Is that how you're supposed to seem after a two-week honeymoon in Fiji?"

My sister-in-law wrinkles her nose. "Our trip was a wonderful balance of physical activity and relaxation."

"Keeley! Not what I meant."

She laughs heartily. "We need to have a baby, remember? Come in, Sera."

Along with getting married, my brother is required to have a son to carry on the family name. Better him than me. I want to fall in love on my timeline, not one created by my father's last wishes, twisted though they may be for Lex. Ideally, my brother can change the bylaws of the company. Right now, only men are allowed to run Celt Industries. Ironically, it's our mother who is preventing the change. Cecile Soren is using her power to maintain the tiniest of holds on the company. The kicker is she's been divorced from my father for years. I'm surprised Baldwin Soren allowed my mother to keep her vote.

"Hi, Sera." Lex emerges from the kitchen area. The chef's kitchen is absolutely his domain despite Keeley owning a bakery with two locations.

"You're as tan as your wife," I state.

"No comment."

"Ewww, bro."

He laughs and then hugs me. "Everyone else is in the dining room."

That explains the noise echoing down the hall. My sisters, Ellery and Sky, are here with their three children. My youngest sister, Waverly, has returned to college. She's in a graduate program for Data Science for Public Policy at Georgetown. The shortest explanation is she wants to work in the legislature creating policies, which may become laws.

I frown. "Am I late?"

"No. They were early… quite early. Something about seeing us and the house."

"Fair enough. Before it gets too crazy, do you have any openings in your schedule in the next week to chat about my options? I have a few ideas I want to float by you."

"Sure." Even though it's a weekend and outside his normal boundaries, Lex plucks his phone from his pocket. "I have time on Tuesday morning or Wednesday late afternoon."

"I'll take Wednesday."

His phone makes a little beep, and he says, "All set. For my reference, what is this about?"

"My trust mostly. I have a business I want to purchase, perhaps some real estate as well."

"Good for you. You are well ahead of schedule."

I won't gain access until next year. "I know. I want to be prepared."

My brother acknowledges my statement and adds, "I need to check on the quiche. We'll be in soon."

I join my sisters in the dining area and greet my nieces and nephew. A chorus of hellos and hugs circle the room. I catch up with my sisters.

Elle and Sky are both blonde with light blue eyes and pale complexions. Wave has dark red tresses and striking green eyes. I don't know how we didn't see the lack of resemblance sooner, especially for Waverly. I can get past the open marriage aspect. If that was what my parents agreed on, fine with me and none of my business. The deceit makes me cringe. Our mother's lies impacted me and my siblings for years and will continue to do so for many to come, especially, if my sisters are cut off. I shake away my thoughts of my mother for now.

We take seats around the table and dig into the feast. If I didn't know better, I would say the caterer is exceptional. Truth is, Lex cooked our meal, except for the pastries Keeley made. He's the humblest billionaire I've ever met. For the most part, I'm similar. The reality is I'm not as rich as Lex, but I could be soon.

We purposely avoid talking about our mother and the trust issue during the meal at Lex's request. I don't blame him. He's in charge and needs to clean up the mess left behind. Instead, we chat about sports and my niece and nephews' upcoming school events.

Rather than go straight home after our meal, I park in the lot of the beach a few miles from Lex and Keeley's home. The quiet stretch of beach is devoid of people except a single person and a dog on the opposite end of the sand. It's chilly today, and the ocean breeze decreases the temperature more.

Watching the waves roll in and out is soothing. Since my life was upended, I take additional time for purposeful mediation. True, I'm not going to lose everything, but gaining a billion-dollar fortune isn't all roses either despite the adage money can fix everything. I suppose the statement is accurate. However, the number of zeroes in your bank account affects each aspect of life. Survival is easier. I don't have to worry about food or shelter and likely never will in my lifetime. Yet, once people learn you have a seemingly endless pot of money, the requests begin, as does the race to determine who is real. It's one of the reasons I chose to stay single. Although I'm rethinking the premise after seeing Lex find love and happiness with Keeley, despite his billions and familial pressure.

I've done the apps and blind date route. There are two other options: Asking one of my sisters to find me a date, and sheer chance that I run into the man of my dreams.

Me: Hey!

Sky: You good?

Me: Yeah. Do you happen to have any single friends?

Sky: You want me to set you up?

Me: Yes and no. My efforts are failing.

Sky: Give me a little time. I've got you.

Me: Love you lots.

Sky: Love you lots more.

Despite our parentage differences, Elle, Sky, and Wave are my sisters. Always have been and always will be. The sad part is the inequity that might be forthcoming because they aren't full siblings. That makes me angry. I'm grateful it isn't on my plate to figure out how to handle our father's wishes. The deeper question for my sisters is whether they want to know who their biological father is or not.

I inhale the salty air once again and retreat to my SUV. I don't spend my money on flashy things. My car is about five years old and in excellent condition. My daily commute is slightly less than a mile. Typically, I walk to and from work. I suppose my loft is pricey, but it's in a multi-use building owned by a Celt subsidiary with a small boutique on the main floor. The location overlooks a small inlet in Mystic Cove. That's how my father decreased the impact of my living expenses. He bought the building and rented it out to the boutique. I would gather my carrying costs are the taxes and utilities only.

The next morning, I walk to Coffee & Confections. Before Lex and Keeley married, I would frequent her café at least once a week. Now, I'm here two or three times.

"Morning. How can I help you, Sera?" Dylan asks. He's been working for Keeley for at least a year now.

"Hi. I'll take a caramel latté and the breakfast sandwich with ham."

"Sure thing."

After ordering, I slip down the hall and wave to my sister-in-law. She's on the phone, so I retreat and wait for my food. Like Lex, Keeley is determined to continue running her business. It's admirable, especially considering she had to scrape and claw her way to success.

With my egg sandwich in hand, I stroll down the block to Seaside Books. It's an expansive indie bookstore owned by an eccentric spinster named Annette Cummings. She's fended off numerous requests to purchase her building and business. Anne always politely says no. I'm the manager and work at least five days a week and have since graduating from college. I have a father-approved dual degree in business management and marketing, but there wasn't a position at Celt then. Since having a job was my only trust requirement, I took one I loved rather than one at our family business that I might hate.

I unlock the side door and flick on the lights. Shelves upon shelves of fantastic adventures are illuminated instantly. Books were my escape when I was younger. I suppose they still are. Each of us was sent to boarding school from seventh grade on. I loathed the years I was there alone. At any given time up to three Soren children were on campus. My high school years were hellish because Waverly enrolled at a different school. She knew her career path much earlier than most. I don't blame her. Instead, I withdrew into the literary world of imagination.

At precisely nine, I unlock the front door. A young woman and her son were patiently waiting to enter.

"Good morning."

"Hello." Her greeting is soft and meek.

"Is there anything I can assist you with?"

The mother shakes her head and adds, "We're looking for the children's section."

I crouch and greet the little boy. If I had to guess he's approximately four. "Who is your favorite character?"

"Stitch," he replies. Then he gazes up at his mother, moves a bit closer, and whispers, "and Bluey."

I chuckle. "Right this way."

He follows me without hesitation. Minutes later, he's sitting on the plush rug in the kids' reading section with a stack of books.

"Thank you," she whispers.

"My pleasure. I'll be around if he needs more options."

The young woman smiles. "I doubt it."

Twenty minutes later, the woman and her son check out and leave the store. Anne breezes in at the same time.

"Good morning."

"Same to you."

She disappears into her office, and I don't see her for hours. In the meantime, I stock the new arrivals and prepare flyers for our next book signing. A local author is presenting the history of an adjacent town. I walk down the narrow hall toward Anne's office.

Given the volume of her normally level voice, I overhear, "I'm not selling to some big corporation for it to be shuttered within six months. Good day!"

I take a settling breath and knock on the doorframe. That explains why I could hear her clearly—it's open.

"Heading out for lunch?" she asks.

I nod.

"I'm on my way to the front. Thank you."

"You're welcome."

Over the years, I've tried to befriend Anne. My efforts have failed. She's strict about keeping our relationship employer/employee. Her decision isn't ideal in my opinion, but she's the boss. The rest of my workday is evenly paced. I bring home some new books and crash. I'm looking forward to meeting with my brother to discuss my future plans.

Two days later, I arrive at the corporate office for my meeting with Lex. I'm grateful he could fit me in so soon. I'm sure he's swamped after his honeymoon.

His assistant, Andrew, who is always perfectly dressed, greets me. "Good afternoon, Miss Soren. Mr. Soren is running a little behind. Would you care for a beverage or snack?"

I'm not used to being served. While I stand to inherit a boatload of money soon, it won't change my life. I have everything I need and most of the things I want.

"Sera is fine. A bottled water would be great."

"Please have a seat. I'll be right back."

I comply and sit on the plush sofa outside Lex's office. I can hear him shouting to whomever he's speaking with on the phone. "I don't care. Find her!"

Normally, I would be concerned with his tone and words. There's only one her he could be talking about, and quite frankly, I'm not a big fan of our mother.

Andrew returns with my water and sits at his desk.

"Any chance you know who my brother is speaking with?"

He turns his attention to the computer, presumably to Lex's calendar. "He had a call scheduled with Blackthorne Security."

I nod and add, "Thank you." Blackthorne has been working with my family for a few years. Mostly at Lex's behest to locate Keeley's siblings and check security for their residential holdings. Their private investigator is top-tier.

The heavy office door swings open, and my brother appears in the opening.

"Hi, Sera. Sorry for my tardiness."

We hug, and he closes the door with a snick.

"How can I help?" he asks.

"If you want to reschedule, I can wait."

He drags his fingers through his hair. "No. We need to chat. Why don't you share what you're looking for and then I'll update you."

"That sounds ominous."

He shrugs and continues to stare out the large window toward the scenic view.

I push on. "First, how is married life?"

A huge smile appears on his chiseled face. "Worth the wait. It would've killed me if I chose one of Mom's Stepford candidates."

"Keeley is amazing."

"She is. What are you thinking?"

"I want to chat about my trust. There are a few properties I desire to invest in and or purchase."

He faces me with a raised eyebrow. "Specifically?"

"You look surprised," I state.

"A little. We are the same as far as our view of money."

"Yes and no. I don't have as much access as you... yet. You've been able to use your trust for over eight years now. I'm just getting started."

"Fair. Please go on," he states while sitting across from me.

"I want to buy my loft and the bookstore."

He steeples his fingers in front of him. It's his signature move when he's contemplating. "The building or the business for the store?"

"At least the business. The profit margin is good year after year. Anne is getting up there in age, and I don't want to lose that piece of the community. There isn't another indie store for about thirty miles in both directions."

"We can certainly look into both. Your loft is owned by a subsidiary of Celt. I can research how to facilitate the transfer. Do you want to change the tenant?"

"Not necessarily."

"Okay. What else?"

I'm overjoyed that he's actually hearing my requests. The last time I wanted to do something with my trust fund, my father shot me down as too young, dumb, and impetuous to know if it was a good deal or not. Those descriptors were to hide the one he really felt mattered… woman. My father wasn't awful, as in he didn't abuse me. College was meant for me to find an appropriate husband, not the education I also gained. None of us were supposed to work for a living and not at Celt. Once we were married, presumably we could be unemployed and our husbands would care for us. Then when the trust distributions were due, we would have even more money. Ellery fought tooth and nail for her job. The reality is my father gave her a ceiling by requiring all-male succession. Then again, she isn't his daughter either.

"I need a recommendation for a money manager."

"Did you ever meet Lily Cappelli, now DeGaetano?"

"Elle's friend from college?"

"That's her. I can connect you."

Nice. Someone I kind of know already. "That is all I have for now, I guess. Actually, the "her" you were shouting about earlier. Was that Mom?"

Lex drops his head and looks direct at me. "Yeah. She took off to parts unknown with her latest sugar daddy."

"Why do you need to see her?"

"I'm limited with the moves I can make until she acknowledges removal from the board."

I wrinkle my nose. "You think it's intentional?"

"Absolutely. It's the only sliver of power she has. Avoiding a public court battle would be ideal."

"Has Alannah found anything helpful?"

"She's consulting with Dad's probate attorney. The harsh reality is Baldwin Soren had two children. Us."

"Are our sisters getting cut off completely?" Awful. My stomach lurches thinking about it.

His forehead scrunches up briefly. "Elle and Sky already have access to their trusts. As the trustee, I'm barred from adding additional funds because—"

"Mom was unfaithful."

Lex lifts a shoulder and drops it. "I don't like it any more than you do. At least initially, Dad believed they were monogamous. It wasn't until he learned about Elle and Sky that our parents struck an agreement allowing them to both have lovers but remain married. I have been paying for Wave's expenses from my personal assets. Alannah and Attorney Alton have differing views on the provisions of the will and trust documents."

"Let me guess. Alton thinks only you and I should inherit and our sisters are cut off. Alannah's opinion differs. Elle and Sky can keep what they have. Wave gets nothing. You and I split the rest?"

"You're on point."

I could be worth hundreds of billions. Holy fuck! "When will this be determined?"

"Not sure. I'm confident your trust will be available on your birthday. We can work on your plans in the meantime. The rest is going to take a while. Plus, there's the whole baby watch as well."

"I don't love this. They're our sisters. You shouldn't need to rush having a kid."

"I don't either. I'm looking at all angles. At a minimum, I would like to give Wave the same as Elle and Sky. It would be termed a gift, so it's tricky.

"Massive gift to Wave."

He tilts his head in question. "You don't agree?"

"I mean exactly what I said, it's a huge amount. Legally you can't just give it away. In a perfect world, we get to share the entire company with our sisters. Realistically, I would want to find a way to give Wave at least her trust value. Please use equal funds from my money to pay her expenses until we figure this out. You shouldn't have to carry Wave alone. What do you want to change?"

"I appreciate the offer. I'll consider it. The gained interest on my personal trust will easily cover her for now. I want to change male succession for starters and the requirement that the CEO is the majority shareholder. It's not how most large corporations are run."

"Public ones, sure. Not family-owned like ours."

"True. Also, I think you should get a seat at the table."

"Seriously?" Inwardly, I remind myself that Lex isn't like our father. He doesn't subscribe to male-centric ideas of societal norms. I'm grateful our caretakers when we were young fostered that belief in him.

"Why wouldn't I? I planned to request it for all my sisters but then…."

"Mom happened."

He shakes his head. "Yes."

"Thank you. Dad would never."

He rounds his desk and hugs me. "I know."

There's a sharp knock on the door.

Lex releases me and quips, "I guess our time is up. Come in."

Andrew steps into the office with a stack of files. "Your next appointment has arrived."

"We're wrapping up."

Lex's assistant leaves, and we finish talking.

He continues, "I'll have reports compiled for you about each aspect of both purchases with and without the real estate. Also, I'll reach out to Lily for you. She hates the phone, so expect an email."

"Woman after my own heart."

Lex laughs. "When I learn more about the inheritance issue, I'll share. We need to find our mother and obtain a signature. I'm confident she will attempt to use it as a bargaining chip."

"Don't give her anything more."

My brother frowns. "I agree with you to a point. We have access to enough funds to fund a small country. If I thought a certain sum would fix the problem, I would part with it. Hands down."

"Same, except you know our mother will keep asking for more."

His shoulders slump under the heavy weight of our family drama. "I do." Unfortunately, navigating the disaster our parents created is mostly his to bear because he's the oldest and only son.

I leave the corporate office and sit in my SUV for a moment, going over his words in my mind. The sheer fact I may inherit that much terrifies me. The amount in my trust was enough for caution and living on easy street with minimal effort. Not for my safety but for my simple way of life. Can my net worth rival Warren Buffet's and everything remain the same? I'm not so sure.

CHAPTER THREE

ASHTON

"Are you kidding me?" I scrub my hand through my hair.

"I wish I was," my father states. "We need to find at least two new lucrative locations. We've been losing money for the last three years." Mitchell Calloway is a stout man. He built Calloway Investments while my mother, Sally, raised my brother and me. She was also the perfect CEO wife, handling business dinners and the like. Their marriage is solid. I hope to find a similar bond for myself one day.

My family owns and operates numerous businesses, including convenience stores, car washes, and a string of independent retailers on the East Coast. Our portfolio includes mid-range to high-end boutiques, a few florists, and a handful of booksellers. I handle the first two types while my older, less savvy brother, Howie, manages the latter. My father is the director at an investment banking firm based in New York City and has oversight on family holdings.

"Why do I have to clean up his messes?"

"He's lazy. I would fire him, but then he wouldn't be doing anything to support the company. Why you? We both know you'll replace me, not Howie."

Frustrated, I pace the length of my father's desk. His office is modern for a guy his age. The desk and seating are angular and uncomfortable. I think his furniture choice was purposeful to keep his meetings short and to the point.

Unfortunately, he's right. My family is worth hundreds of millions of dollars. Only my brother flaunts our wealth with luxury cars, real estate, and designer threads. Neither I nor my parents are ostentatious in our lifestyle. We have modest homes and cars. While we opt for quality clothing, we aren't label hounds like my brother.

Through high school, everyone knew who my parents were and our status. I realized early on I didn't want "Richie Rich" stamped on my forehead. That descriptor comes with others, including lazy, dumb, entitled, and a mark for girls seeking to level up their future engagement ring. One woman like that was enough. Since college, I have used my middle name and maintained a humble profile. I want what every rich guy desires—a woman who doesn't see my money first. Finding her hasn't been easy. Good thing I only have one high-maintenance babe in my life. Penny is my Whoodle. The breed is a cross of a wheaten terrier and a poodle. She's my partner in crime these days.

I stop walking, turn to my father, and ask, "What do we need?"

He raises his hand, urging me to sit in one of his uncomfortable chairs. I politely decline. Plus, I process issues better on my feet, at least businesswise.

"As I said earlier, I need at least two locations." He points to the Bankers Box on the credenza to his right. "That is the most recent information Howie compiled. I don't have any idea how thorough or good it is. Chances are it's shit."

Damn it! "Great. I appreciate the homework. Do you have a preference for these locations?"

"No. Find me two indies with a good profit margin."

"Are you looking to buy the building, the business, or both?" If my recollection is correct, about seventy-five percent of the time we own both.

"I'm more concerned with balance in that part of the company. Your half is performing well year over year. Howie's not so much," he replies.

"Who is handling my current responsibilities while I bail out Howie?"

"You." His response is blunt and unwavering.

My father's faith in me is nice, but he's asking a lot of one person. "When are you telling Howie he's being paid to do nothing?" Managing my workload and his will be challenging, especially while traveling.

My father shakes his head. "Before the close of business. I'm going to assign him to a desk and keep him busy with bullshit projects. When you finish, I'm going to demote him."

My first inclination is sympathy for Howie. My entitled brother is a single dad, which makes what my father is asking me to do suck even more. Nina, who is ten, deserves a happy, stable home. To get it, she'll likely end up with her mother. Christine isn't a bad person. However, her and Howie mix as well as oil and water.

The emotion passes nearly instantly. Howie doesn't care about earning his paycheck, only that it's deposited every two weeks. "What is the timeframe?"

"Nine months." His answer is shaky.

"So six?"

Mitchell Calloway draws his mouth into a straight line. "Ideally, yes. If you find a business quickly, you could push to one year."

"Is liquidation an option?"

He shakes his head. "Maybe. If that is the best bottom line, what would you replace it with?"

"No idea… yet. It may not be profitable. I have to get through that box. If you demote Howie with no intention of letting him take over again, I'll need to hire someone. Handling the entire company isn't a one-person job."

My father's head drops. "Understood. Let's fix the problem step by step."

His response sounds logical. I suppose it is, except for the reality that I'm going to be running both arms of the family business alone for the foreseeable future. I rise, take the box, and exit his office. Rather than start weeding through the info here, I grab my stuff and return home. Our office staff is limited. The executives are generally remote given the necessary travel, myself included.

I own a small condo a short subway ride from our office. It's clean and modern with a shared patio. I don't use the sitting area frequently, but it's a nice amenity. When I swing open the door, Penny is sitting inside ready for a walk.

Hurriedly, I change my shoes and exit the building. There is a wide paved pathway we use once or twice daily across the street. It's midday, which means there aren't many others walking. We stroll to the end of the walkway, turn around, and continue back with the shoreline on our right. Penny is the best. When she was a pup, I worked diligently with her training. She's well-behaved in nearly all situations. There was only one time where she jumped on my niece to get at her ice cream cone. To be fair, Penny was still learning her manners.

After our walk, I fill Penny's water and dive into the box. Hours later, my head is pounding. If it wouldn't result in a shouting match and disobeying my boss, I would call Howie and exemplify point by point how incompetent he is. I've found three locations that are prime for purchase in less than an afternoon. He has been working on this project for almost a year with nothing to show for it. That begs so many questions. The first one is why?

Rather than attempt to figure out my older brother, I make a few notes before calling it a day. By tomorrow night, I hope to have a few more locations to scout and a way out of the mess Howie created.

Sooner rather than later.

CHAPTER FOUR

ASHTON

My rental is a little cottage set on an inlet in southeastern Connecticut. I opted for a short-term lease in a central location to scout the business and real estate. The food in the area is excellent, from the coffee shop nearby to the high-end Italian and Mexican restaurants a few miles away.

Nearly two weeks ago, my father dropped this mess in my lap. After my initial review, I found three potential options in the area. My next pass through the research yielded four more. For this project, my radius is about thirty miles. If I need to expand it later, I will. For now, seven options are plenty. Luckily, my temporary home has a nice office that overlooks the water. Neither sucks.

Before beginning my new project, I walk Penny. The quaint town has wide sidewalks and scenic views. As we near our turnaround point, my normally good dog tugs on her leash. I wasn't expecting it, so she takes off.

"Penny!" I run after her purposefully but not hurried.

My fluffy dog has put her paws on the thigh of a stunning brunette, who pets the top of her head.

"I'm so sorry. Her manners are usually on point."

She smiles, and my heart nearly stops. "No problem. Have a nice day."

"You too."

Then she's gone. Her sweet voice and soft curves were impossible to ignore. Her sage-colored eyes met mine, and I was mesmerized. I couldn't manage to ask her out for a coffee. I don't remember ever being tongue-tied around a woman. *None were as beautiful as her.*

I return with Penny, then drive to a nearby seaside town and wander through the center. It's cute and quaint but frankly feels disjointed. There's no cohesion in the business offerings or restaurants lining the bumpy street. The business on my list is a small boutique that caters to women of a certain age. Nothing wrong with knowing your niche, but the mismatch of a teenage girl behind the counter makes me wonder if they are truly profitable. I can only use the publicly available data, hence why I'm aimlessly walking around the store to purchase nothing in particular.

"Good afternoon," the young woman greets me.

"Hello."

"Are you shopping for a specific occasion or person?" Her question is polite and precise. There is no inkling that I'm not in the right place, at least not yet.

"My mother's birthday is soon." Not a lie but my gifts are more of the dinner out variety than clothing.

"Lovely. Please let me know if you would welcome suggestions."

"Thank you." The teen doesn't belong. However, her training is on point as far as customer service. I suppose something can be said for doing one's job well.

I feign browsing for a bit longer before approaching the checkout area.

"No luck?" she asks.

I shrug noncommittally. "Some potential but I have time. Do you happen to know who owns this store?"

"My mother and aunt. Why do you ask?"

"I'm a small-business investor, if you will. I was curious if it was corporate-owned or not." I was aware of the answer ahead of time, but the sales girl is none the wiser.

"Cool. Would you like me to get them for you?"

I shake my head. "No, thank you. Have a lovely afternoon." I exit the shop and meander back to my car. For some reason, my gut is telling me this isn't the business or location to balance our portfolio.

At the cottage, I change and grab a light jacket and take a walk with Penny. Ever since our arrival and my dog decided her manners were optional, I can't get that gorgeous woman out of my head.

We stroll along the narrow sidewalk toward the far end of my street. The weather has grown colder since my arrival, and the holiday decorations are slowly taking their places on light posts and trees. Two houses down from my cottage, the older owner—and his son, I guess, are meticulously placing hooks on the front porch. Painstaking is more accurate. They are using a ruler to measure the spaces. Both pause to wave, and I return the gesture.

We turn right at the end of the street and walk toward the center of town. It's dark, and we have the space to ourselves. When we reach the park where I saw the woman, I look for her but fall short. I'm dejected, which makes no sense at all. I don't even know her name. We exchanged two sentences, tops.

Yet, I want to run into her again. Ideally, I'll muster the courage to ask her out.

Penny and I finish the loop, and I prepare dinner before relaxing with my latest read. Tomorrow, I plan to check out two locations on the same stretch of road about twenty miles south of here. There's a unique bookstore and a jewelry boutique. The former sells books but also has a lending program. A customer can buy a book, read it, and return it for store credit. In essence, for the price of one, you could read your way through the entire thriller section for a fraction of the cost.

Assuming you return the original novel, it's an intriguing model. Something similar is available at most major airports, but the exchange rate isn't as customer friendly. My big question is how often do people fail to exchange their purchase?

The jewelry store is a mother-daughter team. They make custom creations as well as permanent bracelets and necklaces. Permanent jewelry is welded onto the wrist, neck, or ankle. The piece doesn't come off unless it breaks, the weld is removed, or you cut it off. Of the seven I plan to look at, this one seems the most in need of a buyout or business restructuring. The profit margins must be small. I can't imagine it floating overhead for one household, let alone two.

I turn in for the night and wake to Penny licking my hand before my alarm the next morning.

"Okay, girl. Give me a minute." I roll out of bed and dress to walk her. Instead of turning left, this morning I go the opposite way. We're about halfway through our morning jaunt, and Penny starts pulling to the right. It's completely out of character until I see her. The gorgeous woman I can't stop thinking about is sitting on the same bench. My dog seems to be able to find the yet unnamed woman like a bloodhound.

I allow Penny to lead and approach her. My dog sits right in front of the brunette. She's dressed for a workout this morning. Her hair is piled atop her head effortlessly. Her leggings accentuate curves. Ignoring the stirring response in my body is difficult. "Good morning."

She crouches and pets my dog. "Hi."

I'm not sure if she's talking to her or me.

She rises to her feet, and Penny sits dutifully beside her.

"It seems my dog has an affinity for you." I'm drawn to her like a magnet as well. The sentiment is less stalkerish if I blame it on my fluffy companion for now.

A small smile curls at the corner of her plump lips. "Is that so?"

"Yes. I was wondering… Where are my manners? I'm Ashton, and that's Penny." I force myself to focus, especially considering I used my first name. I haven't introduced myself to anyone in that way in years. Right here and now, I didn't feel the need to mask my identity.

"Sera."

Her voice is unmatched. Her tone is soft and marginally sweet.

"Pleasure to meet you officially. I was thinking maybe we should get together for coffee." Is dating a woman who lives in a different state wise?

Perhaps not, but I'm not tied to my apartment. I can live anywhere I want and still meet my work obligations.

"I would like that," she replies without hesitation. "There's a café around the corner called Coffee & Confections."

"Eight tomorrow?" I suggest.

"I'll see you then. Have a great day, Ashton." She takes a step, and Penny follows. Her laugh, light and happy, is as exquisite as her voice. Sera leans down and says, "You too, Penny."

This time my dog allows her to walk away. However, the lovely Sera turns back with a smile and waves before disappearing around the building. I'm excited for our coffee date. Luckily, my boss isn't a stickler for punctuality as long as the work gets done. With a grin on my face, we finish our morning stroll.

Twenty minutes later, the joy from scoring a date with Sera, my first in too long, is dampened by my brother.

Howie: How could you do this to me?

Howie: It's my job to find good investments.

Howie: Good luck.

I shake my head. It took my brother over two weeks to figure out he was being demoted.

Me: I'm not doing anything to you.

Me: Do you really think I want to do my job and yours?

Me: Talk to our boss if you're pissed.

Pushing him off on our father isn't going to do much. It'll take five minutes before one of them hurls an insult and the other huffs away like a child. I'm all in on my brother storming out first.

I drive to today's small village, which is twenty miles south of Mystic Cove and park in a paid lot. I opt to visit Always Custom Jewels first. The showroom area is neat, clean, and well lit. On the right is a wall with step-by-step instructions to create a custom piece of jewelry. The customer can select from earrings to anklets and everything in between.

"Mornin'. How can I help you?" An older woman greets me from behind the counter.

"I'm browsing but would love for you to explain the process you have set up here."

"Of course." She hobbles through the opening and walks to step one. Her name tag reads "Joyce." With patience and detail, she creates a necklace with a paper clip chain and a single letter charm. Interestingly, she chose an S. Immediately, Sera comes to mind. I'm not surprised. She intrigues me. I refocus and listen to Joyce.

"… then we solder the clasp of choice, and the piece is done."

"What is the timeframe?"

She smiles. "Usually, same day unless we get a run of tourists. We complete the work in-house."

Their process is well organized and executed. Unfortunately, I don't need a gift to test it out. From the looks of things, this business is doing well. I'm pleasantly surprised and move it higher on my list of potential acquisitions.

"I appreciate your time. When I need a gift of jewelry, I'll be back."

Joyce plucks a card from her pocket. "Please take this. You can design through our website as well. The finished product can be picked up or shipped." I wonder how delivery works with the permanent aspect. Doesn't it defeat the purpose if you can slide it off? I suppose earrings don't meet the criteria.

"Do you have many online customers?" I ask.

"My daughter would know better, but I would estimate upward of sixty percent of our business is generated through our internet orders."

"I appreciate the information. It was a pleasure meeting you. Have a lovely morning, Joyce."

"You as well."

I exit the store and turn toward Barney's Book Shack. When I step into the store, my inner bookworm screams with glee. The shop is jammed from floor to ceiling with books. The staff member is working with a customer. I wander through the subject areas. They are arranged by genre and author in a serpentine pattern on the outer walls of the location. The middle has a reading area with comfy chairs and couches. I don't see a coffee bar or vending machines, which would be nice additions.

I peruse the mystery/thriller section and find a good array of choices and even a few new releases. Some of the books are labeled with the number two. I'm guessing those are pre-loved. Signage would be helpful. I pull one off the shelf and find it to be in excellent condition. I select two written by Karin Slaughter. I stumbled upon her work while watching *Will Trent* on television. The show is based on the books, which revolve around two cops who were in foster care together. Both possess unique traits and skill sets to assist them on their cases. I started reading the series after watching two episodes.

While the lending premise is interesting, this business doesn't speak to me like a winner. I purchase my books and return to my car. The good news is my work in Howie's stead is done for today. The bad news... my job awaits.

While I love my walks with Penny, I opt to let her run in the fenced yard when I return to the cottage. Once she's marked a few spots, she curls up on her bed in the corner of the office, and I grind through my emails and voicemails.

I save my father for the last call of my afternoon.

"My main reason for reaching out is to give you a heads-up."

"About Howie?"

"Yes. We had a fight last evening." I hear the resignation in my father's voice.

"No worries. He texted this morning. The kicker is he did the work. He didn't see the potential gems in the files though."

"Are you suggesting I don't fire him?"

I scrub my hand down my face. "Honestly, I'm torn. I agree he isn't performing well at the office. If you let him go, he's going to want to draw from his trust instead." Each of us has a trust we gain access to at age thirty-five. The corpus is the business as well as funds from our grandfather. We gain a sum certain each year. When I inquired last, it was in the neighborhood of five million a year. Is it enough to live on? For me? Yes. For Howie and his daughter Nina? Barely. Lifestyle is another major difference between me and Howie. He is loud rich from his Lambo to his vintage Rolex. My niece doesn't choose most of her things. If Howie is in charge, the labels are unmistakable. If it's her mother, it's slightly less ostentatious.

"At this point, he's deadweight at the office. He's entitled to the trust as long as it's part of the corpus and he doesn't do something illegal. His performance isn't going to improve when he's receiving payments."

Good point. "Does he know they are set to start on his birthday?"

"Not sure. My final decision hasn't been made. Depleting the company of his salary and his trusts payments if he isn't earning the former doesn't make sense to me. More importantly, if you need to hire someone, the money has to come from somewhere."

"I understand." In essence, firing Howie is the only option unless I want to run the entire company myself. If it's feasible or not is yet to be determined.

"Having any luck?" he asks.

I update him regarding the investment options and my progress. Purposely, I don't mention Sera. Chances are, my father would deem her a distraction. The fact is I don't know her well. I refuse to admit he might be right if that statement turns out to be true before I have the chance to learn how she takes her coffee.

"Please keep me in the loop," he requests.

"Will do." I end the call and lean back in the cushy office chair. For a rental property, this seems overly comfortable for someone who isn't staying long-term.

Content with my progress for today, I leave the office and make some dinner. The weather has become quite chilly, so Penny's walk this evening is short and sweet. Plus, the sooner I get into bed, the closer I'll be to my coffee date. Perhaps it's the fact I don't know Sera at all that makes this intriguing. Then again, no woman has ever stirred me up as easily as her with her voice and smile.

CHAPTER FIVE

SERAPHINA

The last time I was eager for a coffee date was too long ago to admit. Given my mother's horrid example, I'm cautious. Ashton didn't push too hard or fast. He went right for coffee only. I appreciate his approach. He also allowed me to select the location, which makes me think he's unfamiliar with the area, hesitant like I am, or both.

This morning I opt for Pilates due to the chill in the air. We are rapidly approaching the months of the year when I drive to work. The workout will also help with my nerves. With the hundred, frog, and boat pose complete, I hurry into the shower. Sadly, I need to open Seaside this morning at ten. I won't have a chance to change between coffee and work, so I opt for jeans and a sweater with casual sneakers. Makeup is not my favorite thing. If I wear any daily, it's simple. For major events like the Celt holiday soirée, I hire someone.

I hurry down the stairs to my car and park behind the café. There's always parking back here. Being related to the owner has its perks. As I walk to the front of the shop, the gravel drive crunches beneath my feet. With a deep settling breath, I step into Keeley's bakery. Every time, I'm struck by the delicious smells of the unmatched food. The décor is feminine and airy. Ashton is sitting at the table in the corner.

While I didn't think he would stand me up, relief rushes through me that he arrived before me. "Morning," I greet him.

Ashton chose jeans and a sweater as well but with fancier shoes. He's tall with dark hair and striking blue eyes. In short, he's hot.

"Hi. Shall we order?"

I nod, and we walk to the counter.

"Morning, Sera. Your usual?" Dylan behind the counter asks.

"Yes, please but make my coffee a large."

Ashton turns in my direction. His cobalt gaze is welcome. "Come here often?"

I laugh. "I know the owner personally."

"Fair enough. What would you recommend?"

Luckily, it's early in the morning during the offseason, so there's no line behind us. In the spring and summer months, the café bustles from open to close, much like Seaside. The fall is slower as far as business goes. Seaside gets a bump in November and early December for holiday shopping.

"Are you a black coffee or flavored latté kind of guy?"

He grins at me, and an adorable dimple appears in his cheek. "Cream is a must. Flavors sometimes."

"I would suggest the cinnamon vanilla latté. Sweet or savory breakfast food?"

"My palate needs to match."

"Got it. I would select the apple strudel or cranberry-apple muffin."

He opts for the strudel. Dylan indicates he'll bring our food out, and we take a seat in the corner.

"Ash—"

"Sera—" He drops his head. "Please go ahead."

"Are you new in town or visiting?"

"I'm here for work, I guess."

I wrinkle my nose. "You guess?" Perhaps coffee will be the extent of our relationship.

"Technically, I'm here bailing out my older brother. It's his job to find new investments for our family business. He is underperforming lately."

If anyone understands familial strife, it's me, especially in the corporate world. I was happy for Lex when he left to pursue charitable endeavors in the healthcare field. He decided Celt wasn't for him. Ellery was made for the CEO chair and yet our father…. I refocus on Ashton. "What do you normally do?"

"My role is the same, but I focus on different types of businesses. Howie looks for small companies like boutiques, high-end florists, and indie bookstores. I focus on convenience stores and car washes. What about you?"

"I manage the bookstore around the corner. After college, I decided to take some time to find the right position. I didn't locate a company to devote my talents to. I considered opening my own firm briefly but found I like managing the store. I use my degree for marketing and social media."

Dylan approaches with our order. "Thanks."

"Enjoy!" he says and retreats behind the counter.

"I went to Columbia for business management and development. You?" He takes a sip of the latté first. "I would like to hear your answer, but the coffee is on point."

I break off a piece of my scone. Ivy League educated. Good for him. Interestingly, my mother would probably approve of Ashton based solely on his alma mater. Her opinion is if a man can get into an Ivy, he's going places. She didn't care if it was from grades or a huge donation from daddy. That logic didn't work for Pierce. "Happy to expand your coffee choices. I graduated from UPenn, where I studied project management and marketing." I eat the scone.

"Cool." He bites into his pastry and shakes his head.

I set my hand on his forearm. Warmth radiates through me.

His gaze shifts from my hand to my eyes but says nothing. Slowly, I slide it away, hoping he isn't offended.

I ask, "Is it bad?" It can't be. Keeley possesses magical powers in the kitchen.

Ashton chuckles. "It's the best one I've ever tasted."

"The owner is an exceptional baker. What do you look for when choosing a business to invest in?" Is he examining my store? It isn't mine, but... I hope it will be.

"First, we research the companies from their public image to the category they fall into."

I take a sip of my coffee. Then I ask, "Such as are there three other businesses like it nearby or are they marketing enough or too little?"

"Exactly." The expression on his face shifts as if normally he's speaking a foreign language when he speaks about his career.

"Don't have anyone to talk shop with, huh?"

"That obvious?"

"Yeah. It's fascinating to me. I'll listen." I glanced at the clock and noticed we'd been chatting for nearly an hour.

"Where is your office based?"

He tilts his head. "Wondering if I'll be around long enough for an actual date?"

"Maybe a little." A lot. He's charming, handsome, and interesting.

Ashton smiles, and my stomach flips. "I live in Astoria, but my intention has never been to stay there forever."

His answer is forthright and honest. "I appreciate your candor. I would love to continue chatting with you, but I need to open the store."

"Can I call you?" he asks.

"Sure." I extended my hand, and he gives me his unlocked phone. It's a good sign, if you ask me. He willingly handed it over without hesitation.

I input my name as Sera S. and my number. "Mind if I text it to myself? I don't answer unknown calls."

"Please do."

I send a message and rise from the chair. Our conversation was engaging, and I didn't notice the café filling with patrons during our date.

Ashton stands. "What time do you get off work?"

"I'll be home by six."

"It was a pleasure having breakfast with you, Sera. I'll call you tonight."

"Perfect. Please say hi to Penny for me."

He gifts me a wide smile. "Will do. Have a great day."

I clear my trash, walk out the front door, and turn right toward Seaside Books. For the first time in… forever, I don't want to go to work. I would prefer to continue speaking with Ashton. I unlock the glass door and begin my workday. Ashton was the first guy in a long time who didn't judge my choice to run the bookstore despite being educated to do more. I support myself with my salary, especially since my trust fund handles my housing expenses and my car is paid off. My bottom line will change massively soon. For now, I'm happy where I am. Am I underemployed? Sure, but I refuse to be harried like Lex and Ellery. My oldest sister's stress is mostly from her future ex-husband, but Lex is all business.

A few minutes after opening, a boy and a young guy enter the store.

"Good morning. Can I help you find something?"

The boy replies, "I need a book like Joshua's."

I squat to his level and ask, "Well, let's start with an easy question. What's your name?"

"Ian."

"I'm Sera. Do you know the author?"

He shakes his head.

"What does the cover look like?" I'm excellent at my job, but I need a bit more information.

"It has a blue train and a black train on the cover. Japanese," he replies.

"Right this way." I motion for them to follow me.

The young guy asks, "You speak the same language as my little brother?"

I laugh. "Yeah, it's my thing."

I lead them to the children's section and pull out *Hero of the Rails* by Rev. W. Awdry. The title is a play on words about the main character Hiro, who is Japanese.

"Yay!" Ian takes the book from my hand and runs in a circle around us.

"We appreciate your assistance," the older brother states.

"You're most welcome. Let me know if you need more help."

"Thank you, Sera," Ian shouts.

I ruffle his hair and return to the checkout counter. Ten minutes later, loaded with four more books, they leave the store happy customers.

Near eleven, guests for the book signing start lining up. Then I greet the author when he arrives.

"Welcome to Seaside Books. We're excited to host your signing today."

"Happy to be here." His tone is gruff despite his reason for his presence.

I reiterate the setup and structure of the signing and add, "I'll be nearby in case you run into any issues."

He nods, takes a seat, and signs the interior cover for his first reader. Over the next hour, the author chats with his fans and signs books. The line dwindles near the end of the allotted time, but he's in good spirits.

"I've never had that many people show up before. I owe that to you."

"The credit is all yours. I merely set up the event."

He shakes his head. "You shouldn't shortchange yourself. I'll be sure to share my sentiments with Anne."

I nod and reply, "Please excuse me." I hurry to the counter and cash out the customers. Mentally, I recall that Stacey should've been here thirty minutes ago. She's a young girl who works here part-time. Her attendance is spotty at best.

Once I finish with a few more customers, I check the messages. Sure enough, there's a message from Stacey. This is the third time she's failed to show up for a shift. Staffing doesn't fall into my purview. I'll certainly inform Anne, but I don't make the final decision.

The crowd thins, and the signing ends. I escort him out and then break down the setup. Once finished, I check my messages.

Sky: Are you free tonight?

Me: Kind of? Can you talk?

My phone rings instantly. "Are you okay?"

Good thing the store is empty right now. "Yeah. I met a guy a few days ago while I was out walking. We had coffee this morning."

Sky whoops and hollers. "Yay! Spill all the details."

I give my sister a brief overview.

"Slow and steady for the win. Same for me honestly. I have Lia to worry about." Lia is my precocious four-year-old niece.

"What do you need?"

"One of the dads at Lia's school is searching for a plus-one. Don't worry about it. I'll tell him you're busy. Jack knows it's a longshot."

"I'm not saying things with Ashton will take off, but the potential is there."

"I'm happy for you. Just because I'm not ready to find someone to share my home and bed for the second time doesn't mean my siblings should as well."

"Love you, Sky. I have no doubt there is a man out there who'll fall head over heels for you and Lia."

"Love you too, Sera. Please share how your call goes."

"We'll see." I'm open with my siblings, so I'll likely divulge a lot to them later.

I check to see if Anne has arrived today. She isn't in the office. My boss shows up for at least a few hours each day. Anne doesn't interact with customers often, but she checks in. This is probably the second or third time since I started working here that she hasn't popped in. That is to say, I'm not worried… yet.

I shrug and walk the aisles, looking for spaces to tidy up. The remainder of the afternoon passes quickly. I close up and exit. When I turn around, I'm greeted by my coffee date and his soft brown ball of fluff. Warmth cascades through me. Safe to say we both enjoyed our date this morning.

"Hi, Penny." I crouch and pet her.

Ashton frowns. "What about me?"

"Hello. To be fair, we met because of her."

"True. All set for the day?"

"Yeah. I'm heading home."

"Mind if we walk you to your car?"

"Not at all."

Ashton offers me his arm, and I take it. His manners are on point. Despite barely knowing him, he put me on the inside of the sidewalk, away from the street. Another good sign he was raised well. His cologne, which I noticed this morning but didn't fully appreciate, wafts around me. It's both citrusy and musky at the same time. It doesn't take long for us to reach the parking lot.

"This is me." I point to my SUV.

"That was all too short."

Agreed. "Thank you for accompanying me."

"You're welcome. I waffled for the last two hours whether it was too stalkerish or just enough to show up."

I turn to face him. "Just enough." The urge to lean forward and kiss him swirls in my chest. I don't have a good metric for normal behavior in a relationship.

"I'll call you when we get back to the cottage," he states.

"Looking forward to it." I unlock my door, and he opens it. I close it and pull out of the lot. Should I have offered to drive him home? How does dating work when the end game is a happy stable home? The questions spin in my mind.

CHAPTER SIX

ASHTON

Running is not my favorite pastime. However, this evening I find myself nearly sprinting back to my rental to speak with Sera as soon as possible. When we reach the top step of the porch, Penny lays down. I may have tuckered her out for the night.

Inside, I toe off my shoes and reheat food for dinner. Once I finish, I consider waiting a reasonable amount of time to call Sera. We spent slightly north of an hour together. She's interesting, intelligent, and hot as hell. I want to know every tiny thing that makes her uniquely her.

Before I spin my thoughts more, I dial her number.

"Hi," she answers.

"Were you willing your phone to ring?"

She laughs softly. It's becoming one of my favorite sounds. "It was in my hand but maybe a little."

I sit on the cozy modern couch and look out toward the inlet through the French doors. I need to get propane for the outdoor heater to relax outside for any length of time given the crisp temperature. "Glad we are at the same point."

"Meaning?"

"I've been sitting here for nearly thirty minutes convincing myself not to be too eager to call."

"Honestly—"

"Only way to go."

She inhales sharply. "I don't have any great examples of normal regarding marriage or family. Also, my relationship experience is limited."

"It's okay. My parents are rock-solid despite having issues with my brother. What are you worried about?"

"My parents had an arranged marriage, if you will. They barely knew each other. I doubt they were even friends. In the beginning, I believe they were both faithful. Then my mother took a lover or two. Once my father learned about the affairs, he found the love of his life. At least, that is what we've gleaned from the stories. They divorced years ago without telling us. I have one brother and three sisters. We learned this information when my father died last year."

She's skittish and rightfully so. "I'm sorry for your loss."

"Thank you. My relationship with my father was rudimentary and not very deep. If anything, Walter, our butler, was more suited for the job. My dad made sure my needs were met but there were no trips to baseball games or fishing trips to bond."

"Knowing what you don't want is part of relationships as well. What are you looking for?" *A little deep, Ash.*

"I need to find my person. I realize *Grey's Anatomy* is a television show, but the premise works in real life. I desire a man I can share my secrets with, knowing he won't tell a soul. Having some mutual interests is great, but also having individual ones is essential. I want a partner in raising kids if I am lucky enough to have one or two." She pauses. "That was heavy."

"I asked and agree with you."

"Starting off on a good note. Either way, you're intriguing and fun to talk to. It's new for me."

"Same here." She seems refreshingly normal despite her fancy education.

"Tell me about your family."

I shift on the couch. "My parents, Mitchell and Sally, were high school sweethearts. They've been married for thirty-eight years next March. I mentioned my older brother. Nina is my ten-year-old niece. She's going on thirty if you ask me."

"What's wrong with thirty?"

I frown even though she can't see me. "Nothing."

She giggles, and I relax instantly. "Just joking. I'm almost there though."

"Oh, a younger woman."

I imagine her trying to guess my age. "I pegged you for close to my age. Was I wrong?"

"No, you weren't. Given your statement, I would say I'm about six months older than you."

I hear an exhale.

"Not a fan of a huge gap?"

"Nothing to base it on. More curious than anything. Tell me something fun about yourself."

"Like?" I ask.

"What is your favorite sport to watch and play?"

"Hmmmm. When I was younger, I was a tri-sport athlete through high school."

"Soccer, basketball, and?"

"Baseball. I love playing soccer. I'm in an adult league at home. Getting to the games is tough because I travel for work. More so now since I'm doing Howie's job too. Soccer and baseball are my faves to watch. What about you? I take you for a runner." Her long, lithe body with curves in the right places has been in the front of my mind since we met.

She nearly cackles at that statement. "Soccer and tennis actually."

"Were you any good?"

"Yeah, I was."

I can't stop the next question from tumbling out of my mouth. "Are you still?"

"Haven't played in a while."

I grin. "Maybe we should change that."

"Perhaps when the ground thaws a bit."

I hear the possibility of spending more time with Sera months in the future.

"Does that mean you would agree to a second date?" Giddiness courses through me.

"Yes. When?"

"Are you free tomorrow?" Seaside Books is closed. I checked the hours before showing up this evening. It doesn't mean she's available.

"I am. What do you have in mind?"

"Are you open to me planning?"

"Sure, but I prefer some indication of the dress code."

Practical. I like that. "Casual with sturdy footwear. I'll only promise to hold off on requesting boots and renting an indoor field for a little while." Boots are what soccer players call cleats.

"Deal. What time?"

"Let's say one. If I need to adjust a little, I'll call you."

"Sounds perfect. Good night, Ashton."

I don't know what made me share my first name, but hearing it from her lips with the sexy cupid's bow is exquisite. "I'll see you tomorrow, Sera. Sleep well."

After we talked, I planned our date. I sent two texts, first to my friend who is a chef and the second to a friend who owns two wineries nearby. I met them in high school.

Joechef: When and where? His name is Joseph, and he's a chef.

Me: Tomorrow. 2 ish at one of Jonah's vineyards.

Joechef: On it. Any allergies?

Me: Let me check.

I scroll back to Sera's text thread.

Me: Any allergies?

She answers immediately. *Sera: No. I'm intrigued.*

Me: That's the goal. Sweet dreams.

I switch back to Joe. *Me: None.*

Joechef: Perfecto! Who is this woman?

Me: Second date after coffee. There's something different about her.

Joechef: I've got you.

A new notification appears.

Brax: You're in the area?

Me: Yup. To clean up after Howie. Want to impress a woman. Can I give her a private tour and lunch tomorrow at Braxton Vineyard?

Brax: Sure. When?

Me: One.

Brax: I'll be there to let you in. Where did you meet?

Me: Penny literally jumped on her during a walk. Two days later, I asked her out for coffee. Now onto an actual date.

Brax: Well done. See you tomorrow.

While I don't plan on divulging my wealth—yet—it's helpful to have great friends in different professions. They'll help me pull off an amazing date with minimal notice. If I'm ever able to assist them, I will. I place an order for flowers that I'll pick up on my way.

Too early on a Sunday, Penny wakes me with her wet nose on my cheek. I grumble and roll out of bed. The chill in the air is more pronounced this morning. We take a short walk, and I feed Penny upon our return. With plenty of hours available, I hop on the spinning bike in the rec room. Once I finish my cardio for the day, I down a protein shake and text Sera.

Me: Good morning.

Sera: Up already?

Me: Penny was an early bird today.

Sera: She's super cute though. It makes her behavior forgivable.

Me: True. I didn't ask. Where can I pick you up?

Sera: At the café work? I'm meeting my sister and niece beforehand.

Me: Sure. I'll be there by 12:30.

Sera: See you then.

Normally, it would put me off that she doesn't want me to learn where she lives. Then again, I haven't shared the exact location either. I remind myself that we barely know each other and go with it. Sera is protecting herself. Ideally, it's because we just met rather than some horrible incident in her past.

I eat and get ready for my date. My mind spirals finding ways to waste time until meeting Sera. It's new for me to be keenly interested. So far, our conversations have been easy and spirited but deep. The topics only make me want to talk with her more.

After watching the clock tick by long enough, I pick up the flowers and park in front of the café. My gorgeous date is sitting near the window with a blonde and a little girl.

I enter and hand the flowers to Sera. "Hi."

She brings the bouquet including roses, ranunculus, anemones, and alstroemeria in a pink and lavender palette to her nose to sniff. Sera didn't mention she loves flowers, but her reaction seems to indicate she does. I'll bring her blooms daily to put a gorgeous smile on her face.

"Who you?" the little girl asks.

I crouch to her level. "I'm Ashton, and you are?"

"Ophelia." She extends her little hand in my direction after annunciating her name slowly and purposely.

With a smile, I take it. "Pleasure to meet you. Your Aunt Sera and I are going on a date."

"Me come too?" she replies with hope in her voice.

The blonde, who I assume is the girl's mother, interjects, "Sorry, sweetie. It's adults only. That's why we had breakfast with auntie."

Ophelia's shoulders drop. "Okay. Have fun."

"Thank you." I rise and greet the woman. "You must be Sera's sister."

"Sky. Nice to meet you."

"You as well." I turn my attention to Sera. "Ready to go?"

"Yes. Bye, Lia."

Her sister and niece wave. I offer her my arm, which she accepts, and I escort her to my SUV.

"You look lovely," I add.

"As do you." Her face blushes red. "I mean you look nice as well."

I pause and ask, "Do I make you nervous?"

Her eyes close briefly. When she reopens them, her gaze meets mine. "A little, in a good way though." She sits in the passenger seat and sets the flowers behind her.

"I appreciate your honesty." I close her door and round the hood. I notice that Sky and Lia are watching intently through the store window. I consider waving but allow them grace instead. They're looking out for Sera. I won't hurt her intentionally. Neither Sera nor her family know that for sure… yet.

"Sorry about them," Sera adds on the drive to Braxton Vineyard.

"They're just protecting you as best they can. Ophelia is going to lead a company someday."

Sera tilts her head. "She's just like her father, strong-willed and feisty." The volume of her voice lowers as she gets to the end of the sentence.

I cover her hand with mine. "What happened to him?"

"He died overseas while serving in the Army."

"Please share my thanks for his service when you speak with Sky next."

She drops her head. "I will. On a lighter note, where are we headed?"

"We're touring a vineyard and then having a late lunch."

"Perfect. Up for a few questions?"

I look over at her and smile. "Ask away."

"Who was your first celebrity crush?"

"Scarlett Johansson."

She laughs. I could hear that sound daily and never tire of it. "No hesitation. I can appreciate that. She's gorgeous and badass."

"You?"

"No judging."

I raise an eyebrow. "There's no wrong answer."

She breathes deeply and whispers, "Joshua Jackson."

"No judgment from me. He's an underrated actor and handsome."

Sera smiles and casts her gaze out the windshield. Despite it being early fall and the foliage is nearly gone, she's mesmerized.

"Have you been here before?"

"No, it's serene."

"Brax does a great job. We attended the same high school."

I park in front of the building beside Brax's Range Rover. At least he drove his practical vehicle today. His car collection is one of the most sought-after in the world.

As we approach the front door, hand-in-hand, my friend appears.

"Calloway. It's been too long." We bro hug. Then I introduce my date.

"Please meet Sera."

He stares at her longer than appropriate. The question is why. She's beautiful, but if I know my friend, there's another reason. Brax regains his composure and says, "Pleasure."

"Likewise," Sera replies.

Brax can't seem to let it go. "Have we met before?"

Sera shakes her head. "I don't believe so."

My friend nods and adds, "Feel free to check out the barrel room and the rest of the property. I set out two flights upstairs in the tasting room. Let me know if you need full bottles. Lunch will be served at two."

"Thanks."

Sera intertwines her fingers with mine, and we stroll down the wide hallway. The exterior walls are lined with bottles for sale from floor to ceiling. Along the back are vats of wine aging until bottling. The barrels are mostly aesthetic.

"Interested in walking through the vines?" I ask.

"Yes."

I take a right turn and lead her into the rows of grapes.

"Do you know a lot about winemaking?" Sera asks.

"Nothing at all. I was looking for a unique and private setting for our date."

She laughs.

"Your laugh is exquisite."

Sera stops mid-step briefly before continuing down the aisle. "No one has ever complimented that characteristic before. Thank you."

I lift her hand to my lips and kiss the top. "You're welcome." I didn't plan the kiss, but I want a real one and soon. If the sparks from her touch are anything to go by, a lip-lock may be epic.

"What is your favorite holiday?" she asks as if the gesture was normal.

"Thanksgiving. At least it was earlier in my life."

She stops walking and twists to face me. "What changed?"

"Howie got divorced, and we can't have the entire family together anymore, at least not every year. What about you?"

"It's a work in progress. Holiday celebrations for my father were always centered around the family business. Celebrating as a family with my parents and siblings was never a thing."

"That dovetails with your opinion about being bad at relationships because you don't have traditions to look upon as a guide."

Sera stops walking, and I'm nearly certain she's going to end our date. Then she does something unexpected. Instead, she leans forward and presses her lips to my cheek. "Thank you for actually hearing me."

"You're welcome. Listening is all it takes for kisses?"

She smiles. "It's a great start."

"Well, I plan to keep doing it."

Sera blushes fiercely. "Good."

"Which holiday holds the worst memories for you?" I press.

"My birthday. Our housekeeper, if you will, always made sure we had a cake and a small gift."

I frown. "Because?"

"My parents never felt it was worth celebrating. There were no family parties or gifts. Only Cara made us feel special for a short while despite it not falling into her job description." Sadness over the loss of joy she doesn't know she missed washes over me on her behalf.

We turn back toward the tasting room as the time approaches for our meal.

"When is it?"

"March 3rd. You?"

"August 4th."

"Happy belated birthday," she offers.

"Thank you."

We reenter the building, and I lead her upstairs to the loft area. Joe is lighting a candle on the table as we approach.

"You failed to mention she's way out of your league," he states instead of a greeting.

"True but didn't seem relevant for you." I motion between them. "Sera, this is Joe, another classmate and friend."

"Nice to meet you."

"You as well. I'm only joking. Calloway is a great guy."

Sera acknowledges his statement and sits in the chair I pulled out for her.

"I'll deliver the first course in a few minutes."

"Thanks."

"Any more friends popping out of the woodwork?"

Now it's my turn to laugh. "No. Just the four of us here."

She shakes her head and plucks the flight list from the holder. "Do you know a lot about wine?"

"No, but if Brax makes it, I'll drink it."

"Fair enough. Same goes for the pastries at the café for me. Keeley is amazing. I'll happily act as her taste tester for the rest of my days."

Joe appears with salad and focaccia bread. Chances are he opted for Italian cuisine as our entrée. Over the next few hours, we chat on a wide range of topics from music to bucket list events like the World Series while dining on delicious dishes, including creamy chicken gnocchi and tiramisu for dessert. The meal pairs exceptionally well with the Banyuls that Brax included with our flights.

Joe returns and offers us coffee.

"This meal was one of the best I've ever had. I'll pass on the coffee. Thank you."

"It was my pleasure. Calloway?"

"No thanks. I'm set." I rise, and we bro hug. Joe shakes Sera's hand. "Ready to go?"

Please say no. I don't want our date to end.

"I would like to spend more time with you…."

"But?"

Sera smiles. "Not but exactly. We should leave, so your friends can get back to what's left of the weekend."

Interesting, she doesn't want to impose on Brax and Joe any more than necessary.

"Okay." I offer her a hand to stand. Like before when our fingers were linked together, a tingly, warm sensation runs up my arm. We exit and settle into my SUV.

CHAPTER SEVEN

SERAPHINA

"Where to?" Ashton asks.

"I didn't have a plan other than discontinuing our imposition on your friends. It was amazing to have the entire vineyard, which is closed for the season, to ourselves, but Brax and Joe must have better things to do on the weekend."

"I'm confident they don't see it that way."

I could invite him back to the loft. As much as my gut is telling me Ashton is a good guy, I'm cautious, is all. I'll have Lex run a background check tomorrow. A girl can't be too careful these days, especially with a potential multi-billion-dollar inheritance in the near future. "Give me a moment. I have an idea."

Me: Can I use the rooftop area?

Keeley: Of course. Want me to have Dylan prepare a box for you?

Me: That would be great. Two large coffees as well.

Keeley: Is he hot?

The combination of dark hair and light eyes may as well be my kryptonite.

Me: Yes. We'll talk more after the second part of my date.

Keeley: I expect details.

Me: Maybe. Love you.

Keeley: Love you too.

Keeley makes my brother happy. It's exactly what I want for me and my sisters as well.

"Let's go back to the café. The owner is letting me use the rooftop patio."

"Sounds perfect."

When we arrive, I guide him to the rear of the building, and he parks beside my SUV. I turn to grab my flowers from the backseat. At the same time, Ashton looks toward me. Our lips are a hairsbreadth apart. All it would take is for me to tilt ever so slightly. The desire to kiss him senseless has been ready to erupt since we strolled through the vines. While I ponder doing exactly that, he pulls back and hops out of the car.

His manners are dreamy. Once my door is open, he takes my flowers to allow me to stow them in my car until later.

"Thank you." We enter through the front door, and I approach the counter.

"Here you go, Sera," Dylan states.

"Much appreciated. We're using the patio. Have a great evening."

His face falls, but he recovers quickly. "You too."

"Follow me." I gesture to Ashton.

We walk down the hall to the internal rear stairway. The three-story climb is worth it in my opinion. While Lex and Keeley have a gorgeous new home, it would be hard for me to leave this private oasis.

"You realize he has a crush on you, right?"

I stop near the top of the staircase and look down at my date. "Dylan?"

Ashton grins. "I'll take that as a no. Trust me. He does."

"The feeling isn't mutual." Dylan is too young, and he knows about my family, including lies, deceit, and bank balances.

Ashton acknowledges my statement as I unlock the door to the patio.

"Wow!" Ashton murmurs. There's a pergola with string lights and two sitting areas complete with a fire pit.

"It's pretty fantastic."

"How can I help?"

"There are cushions and blankets in the storage box over there." I point toward the rear façade of the building.

While he pulls out the cushions, I start the fire pit. Then we sit and enjoy our coffee. We're side by side on the cold canvas with no space between us. The heat from his leg is enough to forgo the blanket.

"This was a great idea," Ashton admits.

We enjoy the crisp air and warmth from the fire in comfortable silence. I lean into him and set my head on his shoulder. He wraps his arm around me and draws me closer. His touch is messing with my head despite the layers of outerwear.

Before I talk myself out of it, I tilt my chin upward and kiss him lightly. Ashton shifts forward and sets our cups on the side table. He slides his hand along my jaw, and goose bumps skitter down my spine.

"If you object to me kissing you with reckless abandon, now is the time to say so."

Cue the swoon. "Kiss me, Ashton."

It's as if a dam broke. His lips meet mine, and we fight for supremacy. I wet the curve of his bottom lip, and he mirrors the move. Our tongues dance and swirl. Each swipe sends ripples of heat to my toes. Then he threads his fingers into my hair, tugging slightly, and pulls my scarf off.

Who knew I liked that? Certainly not me. With the tiniest bit of skin exposed, he angles my head so he can pepper my neck with kisses. Containing a sigh is impossible. Forget the fact that I haven't felt like this ever. That's saying a lot about my exes and past dates. Not that there have been many. None of them made the world around me cease to exist with the simplest graze of their hand on my face and the warmth of their mouth on mine.

Ashton travels up the curve of my chin and meets my gaze. I cup his jaw and drag my thumb across his plump lips.

"At the risk of scaring you away, that was…."

"Perfect," I suggest.

He relaxes when I finish his sentence. "Yes."

"Can I be honest?"

"I would prefer it."

I turn and face him. "Today has been the best date ever."

"For me as well. Does that mean I can take you out again?"

I hold his gaze. Seriously, I've never seen that color blue before in my life. "I would like that."

"Me too. However, I need to get home and take care of Penny."

"She's lucky she's cute and cuddly, stealing my date too early."

"I agree, but it needs to be done."

We stand and return the patio to the same condition as when we arrived. Well, aesthetically anyway. My heart and lips will never be the same.

At our cars, he kisses me goodnight and drives away. The imprint of his mouth on mine is still present when I collapse into my bed, reliving our entire date. The butterflies are unreal with this man. Hopefully, he isn't too good to be true. The main obstacle I see at this moment is he lives in another state.

The next morning when I arrive at Seaside, Ashton and Penny are sitting on the bench beside the door. Butterflies flutter in my belly. Perhaps it's soon, but in this moment, I don't care at all.

"Morning, beautiful." He curls his arm around me and kisses me.

The endearment soothes my heart, and I could get used to him being around. "This is a nice surprise." I bend to pet her. Penny's tail wags furiously. "Where are you off to today?"

"I'm checking out a few businesses in the area. One down the street and a few in the village."

"Cool." I wonder which shops.

"Are you free for dinner, or is two dates in two days too much too fast?"

I shake my head. "Not at all. Yes, I am."

"I'll cook for you. Does 6 p.m. work?"

Giddiness zings through me. "Sure. Please text me the address. I gotta open the store. I'll see you later." I kiss him lightly and ruffle the top of Penny's head.

"Have a great day," he replies, and they take off down the street. I follow procedure for the store faster than normal. Honestly, there aren't patrons clamoring to get in, so I'm not worried about the ten minutes.

The morning drags on. Near eleven, I pull out my phone and message my brother. If he's free, he'll answer. I'm one of a lucky handful of people who has his personal cell number.

Me: You free to chat for a few minutes?

I'm not shocked that my phone rings immediately. Lex hates texting.

"Morning, Sera. Everything okay?"

It's kind of amazing. "Yes. Can you have Blackthorne do a background check for me?" We have worked with both Connor and Jake over the years.

"Sure. What's his name?"

"Ashton Calloway."

Lex doesn't judge. "Are you concerned or doing due diligence?"

"Definitely the latter. He's a complete gentleman, and I took precautions. He doesn't know where I live yet. We met at the café and then had lunch at a winery yesterday."

"This the guy who you were with on the patio?"

"Yeah."

I imagine him steepling his fingers on his desk, deep in my business. Instead, I push onto another topic. "Have you heard from Mom?"

"No. Connor's investigator hasn't found her yet either. It likely means she's broke and living off her current sugar daddy. Be prepared for her to reach out to you. I won't give her another dime and Cecile is fully aware."

"I don't have any money." The statement is laughable. My salary from Seaside is plenty.

"Our mother is cognizant of the details of the trust as well as we are. She's also fully aware of the amount you'll inherit on your birthday. I'm saying keep your guard up. After her antics against Keeley, I don't think you'll be immune." Our mother tried to buy my sister-in-law off. When that failed, she attempted to sabotage the opening of her second location.

"I'm not giving her anything. Has Alannah made any progress?" Alannah Craven is Lex's personal attorney. Celt employs a slew of them, but he needed someone impartial and loyal to him, not the corporation.

"Unfortunately, Attorney Alton has swayed her to the dark side, if you will. They haven't found a way to legally provide Waverly the value of her trust. However, they believe she's entitled to one third of the compound, which is worth more."

Whoa! "What does that mean for the five of us?"

"Once I remove Mom from the board, change the succession rules, and Keeley has our child—"

I can't wait for more nieces or nephews. Best auntie status used to be enough. Having a family of my own was always in the back of my mind. I realize it's early, but it seems more in reach than ever before. "Is she?"

"Possibly. We haven't confirmed yet. Back to the trust—"

"Let me be clear with you. I want to buy the building with my loft from the corporation. Then I'll focus on speaking with Anne about Seaside Books. After that, I'll assist to make sure Wave receives at least the same initial amount as Elle and Sky. If that means you and I are creating a trust for Wave, fine. Also, please reimburse yourself for half of Wave's expenses. Only then will I be able to stomach the reality of being a billionaire heiress."

"I understand. I have been supporting myself without my inheritance until recently. It's an adjustment. We'll figure it all out."

"Two large homes at the same time, I would think so."

"She's worth it."

"Keeley is the best thing that ever happened to you."

"No kidding."

The bell over the front door alerts me to a customer. "I need to go."

"I'll reach out when I get the report. Love you."

"Love you."

I pocket my phone and walk toward the front of the store. I assist the young woman to the title she was searching for. The next few hours drag on. Near one and after my stomach grumbles, I note that Anne hasn't arrived today.

Worried, I place a call to the local police department.

"I need to request a welfare check. My boss, Annette Cummings, hasn't showed up for work since Thursday."

The woman on the phone asks, "Is this a normal occurrence?"

"No. She's here for at least a few hours a day."

The police officer takes my information, and I provide her with Anne's address. "Thank you, Miss Soren. We'll be in touch."

Still uneasy, I order food from the café. I wait about ten minutes, lock up, and speed walk around the corner to pick it up. I wave to Keeley, who happens to be behind the counter with Dylan.

"How was your date?" she shouts after me. Thankfully, the café is empty. She wouldn't have asked loudly otherwise.

"Talk later." I grab my lunch and hurry back to the bookstore. Anne hates when I eat at the checkout counter, but today I have no choice.

As the clock ticks closer to my dinner date, I swear time slows down. As if he knew I was thinking of him, my phone chimes with a text.

Ashton: How is your day?

Me: Slllloooowwwww. You?

Ashton: Productive and possibly found a potential business.

Me: Good for you. I want to hear every detail.

Ashton: See you soon. The rental address is 44 Paget Street.

Thirty minutes before I'm set to leave for the day, the police department reaches out.

"Good afternoon, Miss Soren. I'm Officer Sanchez. When we conducted a welfare check earlier today, we found no signs of foul play. However, when my partner did a sweep of the property, Miss Cummings lay unresponsive on the floor through her rear sliding glass doors. She was pronounced dead about an hour ago."

Sadness ripples through me. One day everything is fine and then inexplicable upheaval. Anne wasn't the best boss ever, but she loved this place. Then anger bubbles up in me. I'm going to lose this the bookstore. *Damn it!* I waited too long to propose a buyout.

"Miss Soren?"

I was lost in my head longer than I thought. "Yes. I'm here. Thank you for the information. What happens now?"

"The coroner's office will reach out to next of kin."

"If she doesn't have anyone?" Anne had no husband or children that I knew of but perhaps a distant cousin or something.

"Then the coroner will set up for a pauper's burial."

Anne would be mortified being put in a grave only marked by a simple name placard. "If no one comes forward, please have them reach out to me."

"I'll make note of it. I'm sorry for your loss."

"Thank you." I end the call and look around the store. What happens tomorrow when I'm supposed to open Seaside? Do I still do it? I probably won't get paid. Inwardly, I shrug. Eventually, I will. Besides, I work here for the love of books and marketing, not my salary.

I note it's time to close for the night. Solemnly, I go through the motions. When I step outside, locking the door behind me, I call Lex.

"I was just about to reach out. Is everything okay?"

I round the corner toward my SUV. "Not really." I share the news about Anne and my anger about not moving faster to buy the store and building.

"I'm sorry, Sera."

"Me too. Do I open the store tomorrow?"

"That's a good question. I'll reach out to Alannah."

"It can wait until morning. Don't bother her now."

"Okay."

I unlock my door and settle into the driver's seat. "What did you want to share with me?"

"I received the background check from Blackthorne."

Oh!

Lex continues, "What do you want to know?"

"Like I said, Ashton appears to be a good guy. I need verification."

"Do you want details or an overall picture?"

"Just tell me if I need to worry that he's too good to be true?"

Lex laughs. "Your gut is on point, Sera. Ashton Calloway checks out."

"Thanks. Please wait till tomorrow to bother Alannah. I'll put up a sign if we don't hear back from her before opening."

"I will."

I hang up and drive to Ashton's rental. After parking, I take a few deep breaths before knocking on the front door.

The door swings open, and my date clad in jeans and a hoodie with his sidekick nearly knocks me off my feet. *Hot!* It doesn't matter what he's wearing, he's droolworthy. Too bad I'm in a shitty mood.

"Hi…." His cheerful tone falls off after he casts his gaze over me. "Are you okay?"

I shake my head, and the tears I've been fighting fall down my cheeks. He steps forward, takes my hand, and leads me inside. Penny walks beside me stride for stride. Without care for messing up dinner or sharing his day,

Ashton sits on the couch and holds me until my sobs lessen and I catch my breath. Penny hops up beside me and sidles as close as she can.

Regardless of the reason for my massive emotions, I feel safe even this early in our relationship. Do we have one of those? I hope so.

"I'm sorry I ruined dinner," I mumble before meeting his eyes.

He shakes his head. "Not at all. It'll keep. Ready to share?"

I inhale sharply and reply, "My boss died. I wanted to take over the store. We weren't even friends and yet I'm crying more than when my father…."

"Oh, Sera. I'm sorry." His hands cup my face, and he kisses me lightly.

"Me too. I probably won't be great company tonight," I admit.

"Not every moment is going to be rosy. Some days, like today, are rainy." His statement hits me square in the chest. He is romance novel hero worthy, except he's not a figment of my imagination. Ashton is absolutely wrapped securely around me. "Company doesn't always have to be chatty and fun filled. Silent cuddling is okay by me too."

"Thank you." I snuggle deeper into him and set my head on his shoulder. His cologne is different today, lighter and crisp. My heartrate slows, and my breathing syncs with his. Ashton's hand skims along my arm. The motion is soothing. An unknown amount of time later, my stomach growls loudly.

I feel him chuckling quietly. "Let's see if we can salvage dinner."

Sitting up slowly, I look over at him. "If not?"

"We'll have to see if our pizza palates are compatible."

"Deal."

Despite his assurance otherwise, chicken with orzo and sundried tomatoes doesn't keep when left under a warmer too long.

"What local place delivers the best pizza?"

I give him two options, and he pulls up the menus. "Hawaiian, yes or no?"

I wrinkle my nose.

"That's adorable. Fess up. Do you like pineapple?"

"Blech! No. Do you? I mean no self-respecting New Yorker could possibly like fruit on their slice."

He smiles widely. "You're right. I don't."

I exhale in relief. We place an order and clean the remnants of dinner while we wait. The orzo is a clumpy mess resembling poorly cooked rice by the time we scoop it into the trash.

The two of us retake our seats from earlier with our slices of pepperoni. Well, I sit beside him instead of content in his arms.

"Penny." Ashton gives his dog the side-eye as she nestles beside me on the couch.

"Is she not allowed on the furniture?"

He sighs. "Not normally. She doesn't at home."

I pout on her behalf and smooth my free hand over her head. "Penny is a good girl. She won't do anything crazy."

Ashton laughs. "You don't have a pet, do you?"

I shake my head. "Not yet. I will snuggle them on the couch though."

"Noted." He takes a huge bite of his slice and moans. Seriously?

"That good or that bad?"

"Don't tell Mama Romano, but that's excellent."

"Good thing I don't know who that is."

He laughs and explains it's a family-run Italian restaurant he goes out of his way to buy his pizza from. "I'll take you there sometime."

Future plans near his home. I like it. A lot. Confirmation from Lex, well Blackthorne, that Ashton is a good guy, provides a sense of calm. My gut is on point, and I can let him in more fully.

CHAPTER EIGHT

ASHTON

At first, when Sera arrived for our date and burst into tears, I wasn't sure I could handle the onslaught of emotion. Truth is—even knowing her for barely a month—I would do just about anything for her, including giving up my bed.

We finish our pizza, which is high on my list of excellent pies despite being from the Big Apple. We can debate all you want; New York style is better than Chicago deep-dish.

"Please tell me about your day," she asks with sincerity. Sera seems keenly interested, regardless of the blow to her life and livelihood.

"It can wait," I answer and hold her until she falls asleep. I'm not cataloging how well Sera fits in my arms and the curves of her body. *Liar.* I absolutely am. I dozed off myself. Near two, I wake her and guide her to the bedroom.

Sera is apologetic for ruining our date and keen on driving home wherever that may be. I understand being cautious when meeting a new guy, but it's been long enough. At least I believe so.

"You didn't. Take my bed."

"I'll just go," she presses.

"Stay. It's the wee hours of the morning. I'll be on the couch." The desire to curl around her in sleep was stronger than I anticipated, but I withdraw to the living room before my libido wins over my brain.

Now, just after six the next morning, I pad to the kitchen to make coffee. It isn't until it starts to brew that I notice Penny isn't clamoring to go outside. I approach the master bedroom, which is decorated in modern navy and gray. It's similar to my apartment in terms of style. While I don't want to invade Sera's privacy, I need to let my dog out. I push the door open slightly and find my dog cuddled with the woman who is wrapping herself around my heart more and more each day.

Penny's tail starts to wag, and Sera stirs. Her gaze meets mine.

"Sorry for waking you, but Penny needs a walk."

Sera sits up holding the sheets over her breasts. Her shoulders and the elegant slope of her neck are exposed. She's stunning first thing in the morning with mussed hair and no makeup. She slept naked in my bed? Part of me is ecstatic that she felt comfortable enough to do it. The remainder would wonder about her lingerie, except the sexy-as-hell navy lace bra on the dressing bench leaves little to imagine.

"No problem."

Reluctantly, Penny hops to the floor. She slips out of the room and hurries to the sliding door instead of the front of the cottage. It's as if she knows this morning isn't usual. Of course she does. My dog slept with Sera. I close my eyes and process that thought. I'm jealous of Penny. Chances are her sleeping attire would've been different if I snuggled in beside her, but the green monster still presents itself. For my dog.

I scrub my hand down my face to wash away the image of my... I'm not sure what to call her right now... woman I'm dating or girlfriend? It's been so long since I've been past a first date. We're on four, I think. The number isn't important. I like her a lot, and the more time I spend with her the better. Sera emerges from the bedroom about ten minutes later. She's dressed in yesterday's outfit, but her hair has been smoothed into a sleek bun at the nape of her neck.

"Morning."

"Hi. Did you sleep well?" I ask. I'm not sure how to handle her in my kitchen considering the lascivious thoughts running through my mind. I would like to lift her onto the granite island and kiss her from head to toe. My self-control will win now and in the future until Sera consents to the same.

She twists toward me and sets her hand on my chest. "I did. Thank you for... being there for me. It's a lot to ask."

I slide my hand around her waist and draw her against me. "No, it isn't. I don't know who you've dated in the past, but I'm here for whatever you need. If it means a shoulder, pizza, and a bed, it's yours. No questions asked. If it means a date to a fancy work function or your boss's funeral because you want someone to lean on, I'm your guy."

Sera is stunned. Recovering slightly, she quips, "You kind of like me too, huh?"

I laugh. "A little." Then I turn, trapping her against the counter, and kiss her deeply. I lose myself in her and the warmth of her against me. I miss Penny scratching the glass door. It's easy with Sera. Nearly everything around me falls away merely due to her presence, let alone a heated lip-lock.

Sera adds space between us and says, "I'll get the door."

"Might as well bring her home with you."

While she lets the dog in, I pour two cups of coffee.

"I can't do that. She's yours."

With a grin I reply, "Sure about that? Penny is drawn to you like a magnet both before our dates and now."

"Just Penny?"

I drop my head. I walked right into that. "Busted."

Sera sits across from me at the island. I slide a mug toward her.

"Thanks." She savors a long sip and asks, "Where are you off to today?"

"I have a conference call with my boss, aka my father, and then I'm putting together a purchase package."

"Which business are you thinking of first?"

She's the first woman I've dated who is interested in my work. Hell, she could probably do my job as well as me. "There's a permanent jewelry shop in a nearby town. It's a long shot because the owners are a mother-daughter team, but the margins are good. What about you?"

"I'm waiting on some guidance from my lawyer as to whether I should open Seaside today or not."

Most people would be put off by the casual use of "my lawyer". For me, it means Sera likely has her priorities straight or she already consulted her or him about buying the bookstore. "Do you know how the company was held?"

Sera shakes her head. "No. Anne was uber-private about that even from me. We weren't friends, but I'm—was—her longest standing employee."

"You could check public records. At a minimum, it would tell you if there was a corporation or a limited liability company. If it's the former, you could open the store and have the expectation of payment. I suppose that's true for either one, but you have a better shot with a corporation."

"That's a good idea. I'm considering doing it either way. It isn't about money. It's about Seaside's place in the community."

"I can see that. Yesterday, you mentioned wanting to take over the store. As in purchase it?"

"Yes, it was a goal of mine."

Perhaps I should look into Seaside Books as an option for my company. This way Sera could keep the job she loves. I shove the thought away for a later time. "Maybe it's still possible."

Sera shrugs and finishes her coffee. "I should get going." She pushes to her feet and washes the mug.

"Are you free for dinner on Saturday?" I ask.

Her eyes light up. "Yes."

I could get used to seeing Sera happy. "Perfect. I'm thinking fancy. Does that work for you?" *Say yes!*

"I could get behind wearing a dress and heels for dinner."

My mind shoots to the lace bra I saw earlier, and my brain pictures her in a sexy dress. Every ounce of blood in my body rushes south. I force the image out of my head and reply, "Mind if I select the restaurant?"

"Not at all. I have a sneaking suspicion I'll need to plan the funeral."

I frown and surround her with my arms. "I'm sorry about Anne."

"Me too." Her phone vibrates on the end table.

The name on the screen is "Lex." I release her.

"I need to take this. It's my brother." She answers and replies with one-word answers. "Thanks. Please tell her I appreciate the advice."

"Sorry about that," she states after ending the call.

"No problem at all. Did she help you decide?"

"Yeah. My attorney did a basic search as you proposed and found the store is owned by an S-Corp. It means her estate is in charge." She frowns. "You already know that. I'm not used to having a business-minded person to speak with other than my brother. Anyway, the question is who that might be. For now, I'm going to continue working until I find out who my new boss is."

The pull of her is intense. I can't help but haul her close again. Her frame against mine is heavenly. "Your loyalty is honorable."

"The store is more than a job for me. It gave me a place to land and use my degree in a low-stress environment."

"Exactly the opposite of your family life," I state.

She inhales sharply. "You're one of a kind, aren't you?"

Inner contentment passes over me. No woman before her ever though I was good enough as it. She sees me. "Yeah, I am." I press my lips to hers. The kiss is lighter than before. Otherwise, I might make her late to open the store. "Dinner tonight?"

"Sure."

"Why don't you come to my place and bring Penny?"

"Sounds perfect. Text me the address. Have a good day." Perhaps my support has solidified her opinion of me. Knowing where she lives shows trust. I'm glad she sees me as a good guy.

With another kiss, she turns to leave, and I tug her back again.

Her arms link around my neck. She groans, steals my breath with another peck, and finally slips out the front door. Before I lose my gumption, I take a quick ride on the bike in the basement and dress before my video conference call.

"Morning." His tone is grumpier than usual.

"Hello to you too. What's wrong?"

He purses his lips and asks, "How are things going?"

"Fine. You?"

My father scowls and asks, "Are you coming home for the holiday?"

I thought we were skipping it this year. "Isn't Nina with Christine this Thanksgiving?"

He acknowledges my statement. "Yes. I forgot. Your mother will expect you for a meal on Christmas."

"Understood."

"Please give me an actual update."

For the first time in my work life, I downplay the opportunities I've found. While I'm sure my parents would be happy for me, I want to keep my relationship to myself for a little while longer. Relationship? Defining Sera and I is a work in progress. I share that there is one solid option, which I will write up and handle this week. Otherwise, I'm still parsing through Howie's research and conducting my own.

"Very well," he states.

"Has the timeline changed?"

"No. I don't like the fact there's uncertainty in the company."

"I agree. Please give my regards to Mom."

My father replies, "You should just call her, Ashton. Talk again in two weeks?"

Mentally, I run through the calendar. "Sure, right after Thanksgiving."

"Talk then." He ends the call, and I stare out into the backyard, pondering the slight misdirection in my report. It was then I noticed the light snowfall. I didn't lie, but my brother may have put me in the path of a woman to share my life with. Before sharing with my family, I need to be sure. As if she hears my thoughts, Sera texts me.

Sera: I'm at the store. Thank you again for last night.

Sera: That sounds dirty.

Me: You're welcome.

Me: Didn't take it that way, but…

Sera: Funny. My address is 126 East Main Street. 6 work?

Why does that seem familiar? I wrack my brain but fail to come up with the answer.

Me: See you then. Try to have a good day.

Sera: I'll do my best. xoxo

For the rest of the morning, I work on my purchase offer for Always Custom Jewels. Then I dig into Seaside Books. At a minimum, I'll have accurate information if the time comes to buy it for Sera.

With a bouquet of flowers in one hand and Penny's leash looped around my wrist, I input her address. Now it makes sense. Sera lives above the boutique I've been looking at. Hmm. An interesting twist if you ask me. I could end up her landlord. Sort of.

CHAPTER NINE

SERAPHINA

Inhaling sharply, I push the door to the store. Going through the motions isn't hard physically. However, it's eerie. My feelings make no sense, but something shifted, knowing Anne is gone. My connection to this place feels oddly stronger. I shake off my disconcerting thoughts and finish preparing for customers.

The first of the day is an older couple. Mr. & Mrs. Swanson stop by at least once a month. They have a massive library in their home; at least that's the story they tell.

"Good morning." I greet them near the new arrivals section.

"Hello, dear." Mrs. Swanson answers. She's an old-fashioned lady. By that, I mean she hasn't shifted to modern fashion. Alma wears skirts or dresses for every visit to Seaside. Her husband, Stan, follows the same rules. He sticks with khakis and a polo—certainly no jeans.

"It's a wonder you're open today." Alma pauses and then continues, "We live next door to Miss Anne. We saw the police. She passed, no?"

I frown. "She did. Yet you came anyway?"

Alma reaches into her purse and produces a letter. "Anne was my childhood friend. We had an agreement and marching orders. Her letter was to you. Mine is… it isn't important." She extends her hand in my direction.

The ivory envelope has Anne's monogram in the top left corner. My full name in elegant script is listed as the recipient but without a mailing address. Anne has—had—my address for my paychecks. Inwardly, I shake my head and slip the letter into my pocket.

"Thank you. Was she alone?" It'll help to know if I should reach out or plan her services. Every detail I gleaned over my years at Seaside indicated she was a spinster.

Alma drops her head somberly. "Yes. A long, long time ago, Anne was engaged to my younger brother. He was sadly killed in an accident a week before their nuptials."

I attempt to cover my gasp with my hand. "Oh no!"

"She never sought companionship again. Despite failing to make her vows, Anne remained devoted to Peter. She was a wonderful friend, and I will miss her."

I take Alma's hands in mine. "I will as well. Anne was a private woman. I appreciate the information. It brings up many questions but also explains a lot as well."

"Of course."

The bell over the door chimes, and Lex walks in. I nod, and he moves past me to the counter.

"Are you aware of her final wishes?"

Stan answers this question. "Anne set everything up years ago. Planning our last party is a rite of passage for the older generation. All you need to do is reach out to Niles Funeral Home."

"Thank you. I'll call today."

Alma releases my hands, and the couple turn to leave.

"No books?" I ask.

Stan shakes his head. "Not today. See you, Sera." He offers his wife an arm, and they exit the store.

The bit of Anne's life story from Alma makes Anne more interesting than I ever imagined. Not once did she mention a dead fiancé. Then again, I didn't ask. Perhaps if I tried harder, we could've had a more personal relationship.

"You okay?" Lex asks as he approaches.

I forgot about him for a second. I shrug and turn the letter over in my hands. "Not sure yet. Did you hear any of that conversation?"

He acknowledges me with the tilt of his head. "The tail end about the funeral, yeah."

"I'll handle it later today and get things started. What are you doing here?"

Lex is dressed more casually than normal. He must be working from home today. "I was at the café this morning. I hate when my wife slips out of bed without me waking."

An image of Ashton pops into my head. Is it too soon? We should probably define our relationship. If I didn't want the same type of love as my brother, his statement might induce vomiting.

"That's sweet."

He lifts his hand in front of his mouth like a shield before looking left and right as if we aren't alone. "Don't divulge to anyone I'm a gooey mess when it comes to Keeley."

I laugh heartily. "Your devotion to your wife isn't the secret you think it is."

"Fair enough. Still can't get over her agreeing to marry me."

"You are a little bit awesome. If you tell anyone I said that, I'll deny, deny, deny."

He pretends to zip his lips regarding my compliment. "I was just checking on you."

"Thanks. It's weird being in the shop."

Lex crosses his arms over his chest. "I'm sure it is. Take one step at a time. Let me know the details about the services."

"Will do." We hug, and he leaves.

I walk down the short hallway toward the office. Aside from sticking my head inside, I don't go in here. It was Anne's space, which she made abundantly clear. She left necessary items in the corridor, and I simply handled them. However, the marketing materials for the next signing are against the wall.

I step inside, grab the boxes, and hustle out. In my head, I hear Anne defending her territory. I change the posters in the street-facing window and return to the counter. Removing the envelope, I drag my hand over the elegant A and C in the corner. A wave of anger washes over me, and I shove the offending paper back into my pocket as if I'll forget it's there. Ever.

Shortly after eleven, a few customers stroll in. I assist them in finding their desired titles and accept payment. I keep myself busy between patrons by straightening books that don't need to be fixed and pondering better placement for the new arrivals.

My gorgeous sister-in-law breezes through the door two hours later loaded down with bags from the café. Chances are she has lunch and pastries to get me through the day. I love her for caring about me as well as Lex.

"Hi!"

"Keeley! You didn't have to."

She smiles. "I know you don't have any additional staff like I do. Plus, you need to eat."

Stacey let a message that she wouldn't be returning to Seaside for personal reasons. Whatever that means.

"You rock hardcore!"

She places her hands under her chin and flutters her eyelashes. "For my Soren sisters and my brothers, I always will." The layer of sadness in her voice from her own sister, Fionola, failing to show up for her year after year is heartbreaking. It's part of the reason I refuse to leave Wave out in the cold. She deserves the same as Elle and Sky at minimum. Keeley sets out a bagel sandwich with turkey and pesto, jalapeño chips, and raspberry iced tea. Don't knock the combination until you try it.

"I'm sure you aren't in a great place because of your boss, but… spill some details about the guy."

I can't stop the smile from blooming on my face.

"I already like him for you. He makes you grin with the mere mention of him."

"I didn't think men like him existed outside of Lex. He's quite similar to my brother. Ashton is well-mannered, attentive, and charming."

"I assume he's hot too?"

"Hands down. His eyes are an indescribable shade of blue that morphs based on the color of his shirt."

"I'm crazy happy for you, Sera. Does he know?"

She doesn't need to say it aloud. Keeley means is he aware of the power my last name carries.

"Not yet. I'm not even sure how to bring it up. A statement like 'Oh, by the way, I'm worth billions of dollars' isn't the best plan."

"Is there one?"

She has a point. "Probably not. The head in the sand approach seems to be working."

"If the situation were reversed, how would you feel?" Keeley asks in a matter-of-fact tone.

"That's the thing. I like him. The guy he is. He could be rich or broke. His bank balance doesn't matter to me in the slightest. Although from his profession and the fact he works with his family investing in small businesses, I can safely surmise he's doing okay for himself."

Keeley purses her lips and starts to speak but refrains.

"Do you know something I don't?"

She shakes her head. "No. Just looking out for you is all."

"I love you, sis."

"Right back at ya." Keeley hugs me and exits the store.

Before I can talk myself out of it, I call the funeral home. The instant someone answers, I hang up. The hollow in my stomach threatens to swallow me whole. It makes little sense to me that I can't handle this detail. Anne was standoffish at worst and marginally civil at best. I suppose the reality of losing Seaside is more in focus. She had no one besides herself. I may not be able to purchase this place after all. That makes me sad and angry at the same time.

After a deep breath, I press redial and begin the process of setting up my boss's funeral. The call doesn't take long. When Mrs. Swanson indicated it would be simple, she was close to correct. Anne's services are set for next Tuesday. The single action item for me is the flowers. Given the time, I resolve to reach out tomorrow after asking Ashton where he ordered my bouquets.

I check the locks in the rear, shut off the lights, and exit the store. Only now does it dawn on me that Stacey may be in the dark about Anne or her work requirements. I consider checking the office more thoroughly but walk to my SUV instead. Tomorrow is another day.

When I reach my loft, I remove my shoes and survey the space. As the type of living space would indicate, everything is out in the open. My style is modern with cozy accessories like the textured blanket and pillows on my couch. I chastise myself, considering I slept in his bed last night. Ashton won't judge my home or decorating sense.

I was forward-thinking this morning before I left. I placed chicken in the fridge to defrost. Cara, our housekeeper and chef, who happens to be Keeley's mother, made incredible meals. My skill set is passable. By that, I mean I won't starve. I put the tray with breaded chicken and seasoned potatoes in the top of my air fryer and set out a pan to steam the broccolini.

Right on time, my… dates arrive. I buzz them in and invite them into my space. As the days continue to pass, the weather gets increasingly cooler.

Ashton hands me flowers and kisses me. His mouth is soft and warm. Heat winds from my lips to my toes, then coils around my heart. I could get used to this greeting each day. *Whoa! Own it!* I want to keep him for a while. Probably a long while. Ashton pulls my lower lip between his teeth. Suppressing a moan is impossible. Penny sits at my feet, waiting for her greeting.

"Hi, sweetheart. How was your day?"

Penny lets out a little whine.

We laugh.

"Hi, sweet girl." I pet her and then add, "You can let her go. I babyproofed."

Ashton shakes his head and unclasps her leash. Penny takes off, surveying my home. "This is an amazing space."

"Thanks. Please make yourself comfortable." I return to the kitchen with Ashton closely behind me.

"Sera."

I turn to face him. I'm floored by what I see. Care and sympathy are etched on his gorgeous face.

"Truly, how was your day?" He wraps me in his arms and draws me against him. He's solid, like he spends hours in the gym.

I relax against him and reply, "So-so." I share my visit from the Swansons, the letter, and the funeral home.

"Let's start with the easy one first. The florist is Petals and Bows. It's located in the village a few miles away."

The timer expires, and I reluctantly move from his hold. Wanting to be cared for is a new emotion for me. Feeling as if he could be in my life for many years to come is a little disconcerting but good as well. Keeley's words echo in my mind as I remove the tray to check our food. *"Does he know?"* I shake the thought away and continue preparing our meal.

"How can I help?"

"If you want to grab some drinks, be my guest." I grin at him as Penny prances over with something in her mouth.

Rounding the island as he calls her over, he crouches and removes the item.

No! No! I only have one thing that color. My favorite lace panties in wine red.

He faces me with the garment hanging from his index finger. "Not the way I wanted to learn your lingerie preferences."

My face burns with embarrassment. "Could you?" I point to the steaming veggies.

"Sure." The smirk on his face is hot as hell.

I snatch my lingerie from his hand and hurry into the bathroom. "Oh, Penny!" Before I can manage to hide the contents of my hamper strewn on the floor, Ashton joins me.

He bursts into laughter. "I think she likes you as much as I do."

I freeze while shoving my clothes back into the wicker hamper. "The feeling is mutual for both of you."

Penny is sitting, prim and proper, at the threshold, peeking in on us.

"Do you mind?" I point to his dog.

"No."

"Come here, Penny." She dutifully moves in front of me. I gesture to the hamper and say, "No." Will it work? Probably not, but at least I tried. To be fair to her, I didn't cover it. It was easy pickins'.

We leave the classic space with pink tile and a pedestal sink to finish preparing dinner. I still can't remove the mortification from my face. Instead of leaving the topic alone, Ashton goes there immediately after we sit.

"So, sexy lingerie is your guilty pleasure?"

I shake my head. "It's one of them. How would you have wanted to find out my penchant for silk and lace?"

He sets down his fork and takes my hand in his. "With painstakingly precise kisses."

Damn! As if I wasn't already aroused. Interestingly, he didn't mention it as pricey. Then again, I'm assuming he saw the La Perla label and knows how much it costs.

"Handbags or shoes?" he asks.

"Shoes. While I don't wear stilettos daily like my older sister Elle, I go all out for special occasions. If I need a purse, I borrow from her. She is a fiend for luxury leather goods. What's your guilty pleasure?"

"I pay for a private suite for a baseball game. Brax, Joe, and a few other classmates make a point to socialize together a few times a year."

"Nice. It's awesome you guys still hang out."

"It is."

Silently, we eat. I'm hoping he doesn't return to his question about my day again. I don't want to discuss it at all. Talking about Anne means admitting I may lose Seaside. That notion is heartbreaking.

"Feel like sharing about the Swansons or the letter?"

The same sympathy reflects back at me. "You've lost someone special?"

Ashton shrugs. "Yeah, my Nana. Technically, she was my great-grandmother. She died soon after high school graduation. She was a spitfire every day of her eighty-one years. Her advice was stellar. Nana never said do this and not that. She offered all sides and then let me make a choice. If I selected wrong, she would rehash it out with me and move forward with a new set of options. Always without judgment though."

"What was her name?"

"Clementine."

"Love it."

He covers my hand with his again. "I'll happily share my life's story with you, but perhaps you want to tell me about your day."

I purse my lips before replying, "I was kind of hoping to ignore the cloud hanging over my life. In here with you, it's great. Realizing that Anne wasn't who I thought she was, and the unknown of her letter puts a damper on things."

Ashton lifts my hand to his lips and kisses the top. "It doesn't have to."

"I appreciate the nudge, but I'm not prepared to read the letter. It means I may not have a job and my plans to take over the store won't come to fruition."

"Or... you might be able to buy the store from her estate."

I tilt my head and ponder his words. "You researched Seaside?"

He frowns, making his eyebrows scrunch together. It's oddly hot. "Of course. Finding information about small businesses is my job. I wanted to help. If you decide to pursue it as an option, most of the data is already compiled."

"You did that for me?" He isn't like my exes. Ashton cares about me.

"Yes." His eyes are bright and sincere.

"I appreciate the effort. I'm not used to anyone other than Lex looking out for me other than, well, me."

"My pleasure."

Together we clear the dining table.

"Would you prefer to wash or dry?" I ask. I don't need help, but he would insist.

"Dry," he answers.

I busy myself with the task at hand and scrub the glass clean. Ashton dutifully dries it, even making sure there are no spots. As I near the dishes and move onto the pans, Ashton sets the towel down.

Trapping me against the counter, he presses a row of kisses to the nape of my neck and tugs the sleeve of my sweater to expose more skin.

"What color will I find beneath this sweater?" he murmurs before reaching around me to shut off the water.

I drop my head forward, willing my body to slow down. Each press of his lips to my skin makes me hot with desire. "You should find out."

He's barely touched me, and my crappy day is looking up. Actually, it was better the moment Penny stole my panties. Ashton grips the hem of my top, pulls it overhead, and tosses it to the floor.

Containing a giggle is impossible. Given his love for my laugh, I half expect him to pick it up and chuck it again. He doesn't. Instead, he drags his tongue from one shoulder blade to the other. Ashton's breath on my skin in combination with his lips is decadent. Slowly, he turns me in his arms.

"Black is sexy as hell. You're beautiful." His gaze is heated and welcome. It's been too long since I've allowed a man this close to me. Some people, like my mother, believe my standards are too high. I don't.

I would classify myself as normal. I have nice boobs and enough curve at the hips. I credit Cara for my self-esteem. "Let's see if you're as hot as I think you are." Rather than give him time to object, I add his shirt to the pile. "You should talk."

Ashton is… whoa! His chest could be carved in marble for an anatomical model.

I could wash those panties Penny found on his abs. He tenses when I skim my hands downward. We dance across my home, dropping clothing along the way. When we reach my bed, we're both only wearing our undergarments.

The bulge in his boxer briefs is barely contained. In the dimly lit space I use for sleeping, Ashton drags the strap of my bra down my arm.

"You sure about this?"

As if stopping was a thought in my mind. "Yes."

With my consent, he unclasps my bra and lavishes attention on my body. Swirls of warmth and bliss follow the path of his tongue over my breasts down to my navel and out to my hip.

His steely gaze meets mine from his knees on the floor. No man has ever….

"You okay?"

Furiously, I shake my head. I refuse to destroy the mood with a small truth bomb. My ex said oral sex was gross though he happily received it. "Yes." My reply is raspy and shaky, if I say so myself.

Content with my answer, Ashton draws my matching thong to the floor.

"Please sit," he requests.

I comply. Inwardly, I'm frowning. Before I can process the notion more, Ashton spreads my legs and sets one over each shoulder. A sensation I can only describe as fantastic rushes to my lady parts, brain, and if I'm honest, my heart. He flattens his tongue between my thighs. The thrum of pleasure in my body is a new height. My hands fist the colorful duvet until they turn white. Each stroke and nibble scramble my thoughts a bit more. My core tightens and coils like a spring.

"Ashton." The moment his name echoes around us, my core pulses and ripples with the most intense orgasm of my life. Bliss cascades through me as he blazes a trail up to kiss me.

"Been awhile?" he asks.

I wrinkle my nose. I knew he didn't buy my answer. "First time, actually."

Ashton's response is perfect. I shouldn't be surprised. "I would like a list of your exes."

I smirk at him. "Because?"

"They deserve thanks for screwing up so royally."

"I'll consider it. My turn."

I roll him onto his back and work my way south, crisscrossing his impressive chest and rippled abs. This man works in an office and travels frequently and yet he's insanely fit.

Licking along the waistband of his boxer briefs causes his length to jump. I slip my fingers beneath the fabric and draw it to the floor. I do my best to school my reaction to him. He's well-endowed in addition to being a great guy.

"Sera. It's been…."

Instead of answering with words, I drag my tongue along the front side of his shaft, lick the precum off the tip, and take him into my mouth. With each pump, his voice sounds more strangled.

"Sera, I need you to—" He tangles his fingers into my hair.

I look up at him, and he stops speaking. His eyes are stormy, and their appearance only adds to his appeal. The moment his shaft hits the back of my throat again, he lengthens and hardens more.

"Sera, if you don't want to...."

With one more pull, he bursts down my throat, and I swallow until he stops pulsing. He withdraws slowly and hauls me on top of him.

We kiss until we're breathless and roll onto our sides facing each other.

"I still want that list."

I laugh. "It isn't necessary. The first one was in high school, and the second isn't worth your time or mine."

"Fine."

Soon thereafter, I push to my feet and throw a shirt over my head. "Want some dessert?"

Ashton grins at me. "Didn't we take care of that already?"

I close my eyes and shake her head, then smile. "The sugary kind, not the sexy kind."

"Sure. I'll be right over."

After Ashton cleans up and gets dressed, we chat over a chocolate mousse tart with coffee.

"I'll pick you up for our date tomorrow."

I eliminate the space between us and kiss him. "I'll be ready. Good night, Ashton."

After the door snicks closed, I recap our evening in my mind. I could get used to having him in my life. I'm looking forward to it.

CHAPTER TEN

ASHTON

Damn it! My offer for Always Custom Jewels was handily rejected by the owners. It isn't what I wanted to read when I randomly check my work email on a weekend. It is their choice to turn down an influx of capital for a second location. I don't understand it, but I'll need to move on. The only bright spot is I'll be here longer. It'll allow me more time with Sera.

She doesn't want to admit it, but she's struggling with the loss of her boss. The details from Anne's would-be sister-in-law threw her off-kilter. Hopefully our date tonight will provide a much-needed distraction from the chaos in her life. Although the loss of her boss and potentially her livelihood has pushed the issues with her family lower in her mind.

Is it outdated to ask her to be my girlfriend? Is it too soon? What is the cutoff?

I'm confident Sera and I are on the same page, but should we voice it aloud to be sure? Either way, I pull out my outfit and get ready to spend the evening out with my gorgeous date.

My phone incessantly chimes while I'm in the shower. Concerned it might be Sera, I peek at the screen. My mother. That can't be good. I finish quickly and read her messages.

Mom: Can you visit for Thanksgiving weekend?

Mom: I mean for a meal on Saturday. Nina is with Christine.

Mom: She offered to come to dinner though.

Mom: It would mean a lot to have the entire family together.

Mom: I know you and Howie are in a rough spot.

Are we? That's his fault, not mine. I should answer her immediately, but truthfully, I want to invite Sera.

For now, I don't respond. After donning my best suit, I send Penny into the backyard. Once she returns and is fed, I retrieve a bouquet of buttercream roses and drive to pick up my date.

When I arrive, she buzzes me up. I appreciate the security in this building. It seems extra for the location, but she lives here alone.

It takes me a moment to lift my jaw from the floor. "You're… wow! You look stunning." Her dress is a rich merlot hue with three-quarter sleeves, a deep V-front, and a pencil skirt. I don't miss the sparkling shoes on her feet either. Before I add more, I step into her space and greet her with a kiss.

"Thank you. You clean up well yourself."

I offer her the flowers.

She brings them to her nose. No woman I've dated before appreciates the gift as much as Sera. "Do I have time to put these in water now?"

Checking my watch, I reply, "Sure."

She walks to the kitchen and pulls down an empty vase. The other bouquets are scattered around her living space.

"Any particular reason you love receiving flowers?"

Sera pauses clipping the stems. "While my parents were barely civil, my grandparents' marriage was a fairytale. My grandfather brought flowers home each week to my grandmother and they had an exceptional garden at their home. When he was serving in the military, he paid a neighbor's son to drop them off for him."

"That's sweet." I'll happily deliver blooms daily simply to make Sera smile.

Anticipating having her in my life in the future doesn't concern me. In fact, I'm excited for the opportunity.

She finishes with the last stem and answers, "It was. Thank you for noticing."

I draw Sera close and kiss her deeply. Once we're breathless, I pull back and gaze at her. Her cheeks are flushed pink and her lips puffy. "You're welcome."

The restaurant isn't far away. It's an exclusive location that caters to high-end patrons with a scenic backdrop on a private inlet. The interior has widely spaced tables with soft, ivory tablecloths, and flickering candlelight. Brax hooked me up. Could I have made the reservation myself? Probably. My net worth and his are similar. With him name-dropping, as he's a local business owner, it was faster.

We're ushered to our table on the rooftop by the hostess. She's young and interested in Sera more than me.

"Your dress is fabulous, and the shoes are to die for," she gushes.

Graciously, Sera replies "Thank you."

"Enjoy your meal." The thin brunette hurries away.

I catch myself staring at her while she gazes out at the harbor and then the menu. Sera is comfortable in her own skin whether she's wearing jeans and a sweater or a cocktail dress and killer heels. The soft light shines off her chestnut tresses.

Our server approaches, shares the specials, and leaves with our drink and appetizer order.

Sera returns her attention to the menu. A few moments later, she says, "I feel you staring at me."

"Staring seems harsh. Appreciating how gorgeous you look sounds better. Less… judgy."

She chuckles softly. "As long as you don't move toward gawking and stalkerish, it's fine."

"I acknowledge where you draw the line."

Sera smirks at me and asks, "Have you been here before?"

I shake my head. "No, Brax recommended the restaurant. Why?"

"There are a bunch of excellent choices."

She's correct. The filet mignon, scallops, and the chicken scampi special have piqued my taste buds. "Which are you leaning toward?"

"The chicken," she answers.

"I'm going with the filet. I'll share with you."

She tilts her head as if pondering her words. As if what she wants to say won't be received well.

"Just say it."

"We're at sharing food."

I smile and ask, "Are we defining our relationship tonight?"

Sera laughs. The sound hits deep in my chest. "Fine with me. I'm not seeing other people. Are you?"

"Only one other woman in my life has any pull."

"I'll agree to sharing you with Penny, but no one else."

Before I can acknowledge her request, our waiter returns with our drinks and takes the rest of our order.

"Deal. Well, then are you free on the 29th? My family has changed the holiday meal schedule. I would love for you to join us."

She frowns.

I'm confident her answer isn't going to make me happy. "I planned to invite you to our dinner on Thanksgiving, if you're free. We're getting together at my sister's place. Elle has her kids this year. Unfortunately, I can't join you on the Saturday. I need to work. That weekend is one of our... biggest of the year." She pauses to collect her thoughts. There is no our, and there likely never was, and that sucks for my newly minted girlfriend. I imagine the turmoil in her heart is heavy. After settling her thoughts, she adds, "I don't know what's happening with it yet. I owe Anne. I'm sorry."

I cover her hand with mine. "No need to apologize. I was looking forward to introducing you to my family. Maybe around Christmas?"

"I would like that."

"Me too."

Our meal begins to arrive, and we chat about likes and dislikes. Sera loves fall while I'm more of a summer guy.

Then I ask, "What would be your ideal romantic date with no expense spared?"

Sera doesn't hesitate. "Dinner overlooking the Thames in the London Eye with the lights twinkling against the dark, starry sky. London is one of my bucket list vacation spots."

Doable. "Mine too actually. Where have you traveled abroad?"

Our meals arrive as Sera shares her study abroad experience in Paris with side trips to Spain and Portugal before returning home.

"That sounds fascinating."

"The architecture and cuisine in Spain was phenomenal. Where have you visited?"

"I spent a semester in Ireland. The scenery is lush, green, and frankly stunning. I spent my weekends sightseeing and soaking up the local fare and culture."

"Nowhere since?" she asks while stabbing the second to last bite of my filet.

"After college, I started working and never stopped."

"No vacations or just not abroad?"

I shake my head. "I take time off each year, but I haven't been to Europe or the United Kingdom since college."

"Oh. Vacation is important."

"I agree." Our server approaches with our dessert options. We choose different options to try more than one. I opt for the crème brûlée, and Sera selects the cheesecake flight. Three different flavors on a single plate sound delicious.

Generally, I don't want to be fed. When Sera lifts a spoon with caramel cheesecake for me to taste, I happily oblige. The fluffy mixture combined with the sweet sugary swirl makes me moan. Stifling the reaction even in this setting is impossible.

My date sits up straighter in her seat and stares me down. Heat and desire increase in her gaze as we finish testing each slice.

I can't sign the bill fast enough when our server returns with it. The ride to her loft is shorter than the cottage. Sera takes my hand, leading me back to her bed. She grips the side of her dress and draws the zipper down. Then Sera adds space and drops it to the floor, revealing an unlined red lace bra. It leaves nothing to my imagination. Her aroused nipples scream to be tasted. I tug her close, dip my head, and take her nipple between my teeth.

"Ashton," she rasps, her head falling back and her fingernails digging into my biceps.

Noted, sweetheart. Unclasping her bra, I pull it forward, caressing her breasts while moving closer to the bed. After her bra slides along her arms, she lifts my shirt over my head. She kisses a path across my chest and down my side. Lowering my hands, I dip my fingers beneath the ties at her side, sliding my hands along her hips to push them off. As I rise, I press open-mouthed kisses, alternating from one leg to the other before teasing the hem of the matching red thong with my tongue, then alongside her breast, before finishing at her lips.

Sera drags her fingertips up the front of my thighs before cupping my shaft through my pants. Her nimble fingers open the clasp, and she pushes them to the floor. I harden and lengthen before this gorgeous woman. Sera takes a step forward and moves over me on the bed.

The look in her eyes is hard to discern. "Do you want me to stop?"

"No, I'm… never mind."

"Sera, please tell me."

"I care about you, and this moment feels different, bigger than it ever has before."

The implications of her statement aren't lost on me. "Me too, or I wouldn't be here."

She hesitates slightly before pulling my lips down to hers. Sliding down her body, my hands skim the sides of her breasts. She grinds against me. I savor the feeling of her heat over my rock-hard shaft. With finesse I didn't know I possessed, I roll us both and wiggle out of my boxer briefs.

Shifting to the center of her bed, I murmur, "Lie back."

She reclines between my legs, and I tease her center with my fingers, drawing up from the bottom to the nub and back down again. I plunge two fingers into her.

"Ashton."

Just my name, nothing more, but the raspy and breathlessness are impossible to miss. Her inner muscles pulse around my fingers as bliss cascades over her.

"Condom?"

"Beside the table in the back of the top drawer," she answers.

A sense of comfort fills my chest when I note the box is unopened. Then again, Sera shared her limited history with me. I tear into the box and pull out a strip.

Sera raises an eyebrow in question. "More than one?"

I laugh. "Maybe." I slide the condom down my length as Sera straddles my hips.

She aligns herself.

"Go slow."

She nods and takes an inch of me inside her core. Sera waits until she stretches to accommodate me. She lowers the rest of the way with my entire shaft buried to the hilt.

I circle my hips as Sera pushes down. We meet each other thrust for thrust. I dig my fingers into the flesh of her hips, marking her and controlling her movements.

I'm not going to last with her riding me with reckless abandon like our first kiss. Rather than address it, I wrap my arm around her waist and flip us over. I hold one of her wrists about her head and a thigh up and push into her with steady, sensual strokes.

"Oh my…."

As with most people, my first sexual experience was awkward and not pleasant. Being with Sera is a wholly different level of pleasure.

Her inner walls tighten around me.

"Do that again."

She complies, and I swell more inside her. Again, she clenches around me. That's all it takes. My body shudders and convulses as I explode in hot bursts. I release her leg and wrist, lowering on top of her, burying my face into the crook of her neck. Our breathing regulates in its own time.

"That was…." So many words ping around in my head to describe how I feel right now. None seem adequate.

"It was."

"Did I hurt you?"

"No, not at all."

I push up and move off the bed. "I'll be right back." I disappear into the bathroom and return a bit later with a towel in hand. Gently, I clean Sera before setting it on the floor. I pull her into my arms, and she rests her head on my chest.

"Your heart is beating fast. Are you good?" She lifts her gaze to see my face.

"I'm excellent." Except for the fact I can't stay. I'm kicking myself for not bringing Penny with me.

"Me too."

We remain cuddled for a while before I tilt her head up to kiss her. Instantly, she frowns.

"I'll walk you out," she mumbles.

I shake my head. "No. I can handle it myself. Stay here."

The reluctance on her face can't be missed. I dress and take a seat on the edge of her bed. With a toe-curling kiss, I exit her loft. The entire ride back to the cottage, my thoughts revolve around Sera. No woman has ever seen me as clearly as her.

CHAPTER ELEVEN

SERAPHINA

Each time I wonder if he's too good to be true, he manages to surprise me again. Our meal was amazing, as was tangling my sheets after dancing into bed. As much as I would've preferred he stay over last night, he needed to take care of Penny. It seems soon for us to sleep together. Yet, I want to more than I have with any man ever before.

When I arrive at the café to pick up my breakfast order, Ashton and Penny are waiting for me.

He greets me with a kiss that borders on inappropriate. Truthfully, I like feeling claimed though I'm not ready to admit that to him. The ways he made my body sing is a marvel. Multiple orgasms in a day is new for me but also welcome.

"Morning, sweetheart. Did you sleep well?" he greets me.

I reach down and pet Penny. "I did. You?"

Ashton, clad in athletic pants, a hoodie, and a light parka, looks left and right to verify we're alone before answering. "I would prefer waking up with you snuggled against me."

Swoon. "I see. I'll keep it in mind."

"Please do. Dinner at your place?"

"Yes. Let's do it a little later. I have a few things to iron out for Anne's service tomorrow." I need to confirm the floral delivery and the food for the repast in the church basement.

"No problem. See you tonight." He kisses me again, and they're off at a brisk pace. Did I know he jogs, or is he late because he was waiting for me? Probably the latter.

"Morning, Sera." Dylan greets me. "New boyfriend?"

Ashton's statement about Keeley's employee echoes in my mind. *He's interested in you.* I decide to share and hopefully push off any potential advances. "Yes."

Dylan nods and hands me my order. "Have a great day." His words are short and not overly friendly. It appears Ashton was correct. I didn't see it. Then again, I'm not one to date anyone who is aware of my family drama and wealth beforehand.

I walk to the store and open for the day. For the most part, I'm the face of Seaside. Anne was always behind the scenes. A select few patrons like the Swansons, Mr. Potter, and Miss Estelle were friendly with my boss. Once I finished my chocolate croissant and latté, I placed a sign on the front door. I realize Anne is gone, but writing the words "Closed for funeral" is a lot. Little did I know it was just the beginning of my tough day.

Near lunch as I return to the front of the store, I hear the front door chime. I had no choice but to check the office email. I don't make it around the counter before her voice causes me to cringe.

"My darling, Seraphina. It's so good to see you."

A chill, and not the kind Ashton drew from my body with ease, cascades over me. *Mother.* As expected, despite her alleged lack of funds, Cecile Soren is clad in luxury from head to toe, including a new Bolide Birkin. "Where have you been? What are you doing here?"

"I came to see if your brother is fulfilling his husbandly duties."

Gross. Lex and Keeley need to have a son so he can inherit Celt industries. Cecile gets nothing even if they fail to have a child in the required timeframe. The meddling seems unnecessary.

My mother continues, "Alas, the maid's daughter wasn't at her job. Then I came here to chat about your multi-millionaire beau." True, Keeley was our maid's daughter, but calling her two-location small business a job is belittling and rude.

Discreetly, beneath the counter, I text my brother.

Me: Our mother is at Seaside.

"My what?"

She scoffs and pulls a printout from her handbag and sets it before me on the yellowing Formica. "Did you not see your photo on Page Six? If I knew you would find a wealthy husband on your own, I might have left Ellery alone."

A pit forms in my belly. The title reads "High Value Merger?" The caption beneath the photo from dinner is "Soon-to-be billionaire socialite and Calloway heir seen canoodling at exclusive restaurant". I can only imagine the comments on the website. This is one of the reasons I avoid personal social media. The photo depicts the moment when I declined his invitation for the holiday dinner. His hand covers mine, and his expression is pure understanding and not a hint of angst or anger. I wouldn't call it canoodling but whatever. Too bad they used this image. The one where he kissed me against his SUV would've earned more clicks. My heart rate rises just thinking about it.

"I ask again, what are you doing here? This is my place of business. I have nothing to say to you."

She drops her head. When my mother looks up again, her expression has changed. Rather than glee at my impending marriage to a wealthy man, her face is somber. Then she drops the hammer.

"I'm broke. Lexington refuses to pay my bills."

I can't contain my laughter. Callous? Perhaps. Cold? Definitely. Necessary for my peace and well-being? Absolutely. "I'm not giving you a dime. Sell that purse. You could probably get thirty grand for it."

My mother shakes her head. "That won't cover my expenses."

I balk at her statement. "Not my problem."

"What do you expect me to do?" she whines.

I briefly consider being nice to her, but the reality is I don't care. "I know you aren't broke-broke. If you were, the last thing you would do is come here wearing an ensemble worth nearly a quarter of a million dollars, excluding your jewelry. You have money from your parents' settlement. If you blew ten million in less than a year, that's on you. As far as Lex not paying your bills, that's also on you. You chose to ignore Dad's request to share the details of our family. Truth be told, I don't want to know the intricacies of your marriage. Both of you were unfaithful, and that's as deep as I need to go. You thought you were smarter than him. Well, he ran circles around you, and he did it legally and in writing. He protected his children, not yours. Now, Lex is working his tail off to figure out how to cobble together a reasonable solution. I can assure you though, nothing Lex decides upon will include you receiving any money from him, me, or my father's company. Please leave."

"You would leave me destitute when you will inherit billions," she squawks at me.

"You're mistaken. I'm not doing anything to you. You did this to yourself. Besides, I won't have access to the money anytime soon. Please leave."

"I'm disappointed in you. It's okay for you to find a rich man, but it wasn't okay for me?"

I considered dispelling her notion that I knew Ashton's bank balance before we met but don't. Her opinion no longer matters to me. "The status of my personal life is none of your business nor is his alleged wealth. I can take care of myself."

My mother scoffs. "With your piddly salary from this store? I never understood your love of this place."

At least I have a way to support myself, unlike her who relies on everyone else. Forcing my anger down, I reply, "My reasoning and paycheck aren't relevant to this conversation. Nor do I intend to share with you. Please leave this establishment, or I'll call the police."

Her eyes narrow, and she shifts on her Louboutin heels.

My heart sinks, and I have the urge to hurl. Ashton is standing near the entrance. *How long has he been here?* I didn't hear the door chime. I hoped to keep Cecile Soren far away from him. His gaze is pinned on me. I tilt my head, hoping he understands I want to avoid a confrontation with my mother.

Ashton drops his head and moves behind the stacks. Cecile has continued talking and pushing her agenda. Something about I owe her, and I can't ignore my own mother. She's completely oblivious to his presence. I'm not big on higher powers, but I'm thanking my lucky star or whatever at this moment.

Reaching to my left, I grab the phone, set to dial.

"You wouldn't dare," she seethes.

"I would. I'm in charge of this business. I have asked you to leave three times, and you haven't complied."

"I'm your mother."

"A fact of biology doesn't mend the family you destroyed with your affairs."

"It was only two affairs. If you're going to hate me, you should have all the facts."

"I don't need them. Although, it would be smart to share with your former lovers that they have children you kept from them their entire lives. You ruined my family and my siblings with your selfishness." That last bit struck a nerve. A crack of guilt or remorse widened on her face. "Last chance."

Surprisingly and finally, she turns on her red-soled shoes, which could also defray her expenses, and exits through the glass door.

I exhale a shaky breath and will my hands to stop trembling. Ashton circles the shelves and wraps me in his arms. I'm not sure what to make of his reaction to my mother. Then again, I don't know how much he heard. Either way, in this moment, I'm protected from the outside world even if it's for a brief period of time. Even if he heard every word and will run away from me and our budding potential, being held close in the calm is perfect.

Truth be told, I wouldn't blame him.

I settle myself in his embrace. Time is passing, but I'm not sure how much. Thankfully, no customers enter the store before I regain my composure. Somewhat anyway.

"Hi." I mumble against his crisp Oxford shirt. Then I dare to look at his gorgeous face. His expression is difficult to read. I can tell he isn't angry with me though.

"Are you okay?"

I purse my lips and shake my head. "Not at all."

"How can I help?" he asks. Despite the short time we've been together, I could ask him nearly anything, and he would find a way to pull it off. He would even if he weren't wealthy. That's telling in my opinion.

"I don't know if you can, aside from being present for me."

He presses his lips to my forehead. The sweetness and intimacy warms my entire body.

I'm almost afraid to ask but determine it's necessary. "What are you doing here?"

"My parents also had a reaction to our photo. It was much different than your mother's."

My eyes flutter closed, and I prepare myself for the breakup speech.

He continues, "They would like to meet you this weekend."

"I have—"

He kisses me to shut me up. I don't hate it. "I know. They are willing to come here instead of us going to New York, given the short notice and holiday travel issues. I wanted to check with you before agreeing."

Is that what normal parents are like? Understanding that their children are adults with lives and occasionally are unable to show up when requested? Is this a grown-up relationship as well?

"I would love to join you. Please thank them for being flexible."

He smiles. "I was thinking the same thing about you. This week is going to be rough."

I shrug and drop my forehead to meet his. He's right. Along with the funeral, we're meeting each other's families over a holiday meal. What could possibly go wrong? "I wasn't expecting my mother to show up and accuse me of disowning her. How much of that did you hear?"

"Enough."

My shoulders roll forward, and I drop my head.

Ashton takes his index finger and lifts my chin up until we're face to face again. "Truth be told, I had my guy run a background check on you."

"I did too."

He smirks. "Yeah, I know. My guy and your guy are partners."

"What?"

"My friend Cash Morgan recommended Jake from Blackthorne Security. It appears you reached out to Connor soon after me."

"My brother did on my behalf. Either way, I merely wanted to confirm my gut was right about you. I didn't dig into anything specific. Lex said you were solid."

"Jake had nothing but glowing things to share about you, your father, and siblings. He did caution me about your mother though."

"I'm sorry you had to witness that."

"The parts of your argument I heard weren't entirely news. Like me, you avoided the rich-kid-preferred spouse route. Marry so-and-so to merge our portfolios. I'm glad you didn't."

I smile weakly. "Me too. My family is a twisted mass of lies and deception nearly all perpetrated by my mother. I'll share someday."

Ashton kisses the tip of my nose. "I only need to know the details to protect you from her, if you'd accept such assistance."

It's as if he reached into my head, saw my concerns, and offered to shield me from the same.

"Okay. Just not today or even this week."

Ashton draws me against his body, and his muscular arms hold me firmly but don't suffocate me. He's perfect. I don't mean like we won't argue or things will never go wrong but he understands me. "Thank you for not running."

He grins at me. "I don't scare easily, Seraphina. Love your full name by the way. Plus, and more importantly, I care about you and want to see where we can go."

A shiver runs down my spine when he calls me Seraphina. "Glad we agree."

The front door opens, and my big brother storms inside. "Where is she?"

I shake my head and reply, "Gone."

Lex drags his hand through his hair. "Damn it!" It's only then does he read the room.

"Lex, this is Ashton."

"Ashton, my brother."

They shake hands. Neither of the men posture or have any pretext. Merely an introduction between two successful businessmen. "Were you here the entire time?"

My boyfriend shakes his head and replies, "Unfortunately not. The portions I did hear were mostly Sera standing up for herself and, well, you."

"She won't hurt me, Lex. Money is her only goal. I refuse to give it to her. My concern is what she'll do now with that knowledge."

Lex pinches the bridge of his nose. "I don't see any more moves for her. The single thing Cecile hasn't done is sign the acknowledgment of her removal from the board. It means nothing to her but prevents me from making big changes like adding you to her seat."

"There's only one option," I state.

My brother tilts his head in interest. "What?"

"Subterfuge."

Ashton's eyes widen with wonder, and his hand tightens around mine.

"What are you suggesting?" Lex asks.

"Invite her to the holiday soirée. She'll show because it'll appear to those on the outside that we've forgiven her. It gives her the chance to be back in the room again. Before she leaves, she signs or you threaten to have her arrested for… something."

Lex laughs. "That's dark but doable. I don't know what we can threaten her with, but I'm sure Alannah can come up with something plausible." Alannah Craven is Lex's personal attorney.

"Also, before I forget and the information doesn't impact us, but…. She mentioned there were two affairs. I didn't dig more. I wanted her out of my space. There are potentially two fathers out there for our sisters, who have no clue about them." Part of me wished I had pressed for their benefit, but containing my emotions was more vital. Ashton surely heard that part of our conversation so no sense in being secretive now.

"I've spoken to our sisters about their fathers. At this point, only Wave is interested in tracking hers down," Lex shares.

"Okay."

Ashton's phone vibrates in his pocket. He pulls it out and says, "Please excuse me a moment." My man who unknowingly showed up when I needed him steps away.

"I'm happy for you, Sera," Lex offers. "He seems like a great guy."

"Thanks. I agree. Don't go crazy on him, please."

Lex laughs. "I won't, but I would like to get to know him better."

I smile. "My gut is on point. You said so yourself. He's not like the men in the folder Mom created for Ellery. Either way, he's coming to dinner on Thursday."

"I wasn't questioning your intuition or feelings. Just being cautious is all."

I close my eyes and nod. "Any progress with my loft?"

Lex frowns, and the answer slaps me in the face.

"That woman is still messing things up for me! You need board approval, don't you?"

"Yeah."

Ashton returns to my side.

Lex continues, our topic of conversation set aside for now. "Please tell me if she comes back. I'll see you both at Elle's." He turns to Ashton. "It was a pleasure meeting you."

"You as well," Ashton replies.

Lex exits the store.

I slide my arms around Ashton and rest my head on his shoulder.

"That wasn't so bad."

I laugh against him. "That's only one. There are my grandfather, four sisters, two nieces, and a nephew to impress."

He frowns. "Four sisters?"

"Lex's wife was the daughter of our housekeeper when I was young. Now, we're legally sisters of sorts."

"She owns the café?"

"Yeah."

"Please thank her personally for allowing us to use the patio."

I lift my gaze to meet his. "Okay. I'm sure you need to get back to work."

He shakes his head. "Not really."

"What happened? I haven't been inquisitive lately about your purchase offer."

He cups my face with his hands. "You have a lot going on right now. The custom jewelry shop owners turned down my proposal. My second option is the boutique in your building. Pursuing that doesn't make sense anymore."

"I'm sorry."

He presses a soft kiss on my lips. "Don't be. It means I'll have to dig deeper and stick around the area."

"I like that last part."

Ashton grins from ear to ear. "Me too. I'll be over for dinner later." He kisses me again and leaves the store.

Before I return to store business, I confirm the details for tomorrow that my mother pushed off by her arrival. The last thing I want is my mother in the same room as Ashton, but I still plan to ask him to be my date for the soirée. The idea of him in a tailored tuxedo makes my mouth water and my mind spin with possibilities of taking it off his rock-solid frame.

The wind swirls around me as I exit my car at the funeral home. The skies are dark and overcast. Exactly how one would picture it on a somber day like today. As I reach the base of the staircase, Ashton sidles beside me.

"What are you doing here?"

"I stopped by your place, but you were already gone. I'm here for you."

"Really?"

The corner of his mouth curls up in a small smile. "You are quickly becoming my favorite person, Seraphina. Would you allow me to stand beside you for support today?" He wipes the tear that fell from my eye with the pad of his thumb.

Forming a reply is impossible. I care about him too. No one comes to a funeral for a woman they never met with a new partner this fast unless… I ignore the possibilities to finish that thought. I could see myself with Ashton in the future, far into the future. With those thoughts floating in my mind, I manage, "Yes. Thank you."

When Mrs. Swanson stated that Anne took care of everything, it was an understatement. The extent of my planning was three phone calls, one to the funeral home, one to the florist, and one to the caterer. That's it.

We're greeted by the funeral director and ushered into the viewing room. The room is much larger than I think will be necessary, but as I mentioned, Anne planned each detail herself.

Soon after I pay my respects, I sit in the front row. For the next three hours, a steady stream of people enter the room and leave after polite niceties about Anne. My former boss wasn't religious, so there won't be a mass at church.

Just before the end of calling hours, the Swansons and Miss Estelle arrive. I greet them with a hug.

"Hello, dear," Alma states. "Who might you be?"

Ashton extends his hand. "Ashton, pleasure to meet you."

Alma looks directly at me. "He's easy on the eyes, and his voice is like butta'.'"

I cover my mouth and turn away from her to stifle a laugh. She isn't wrong on either count, but here is probably not the best place to discuss how hot my boyfriend may be.

"Thank you," Ashton replies as the director takes his place at the front of the room. We follow his instructions and leave for our vehicles. "I'll join you, and we can pick up my car later."

Until this instant, the loss of Anne was more about Seaside than anything else. We weren't friends. I would go so far as to say we were civil, which in my book is less than friendly. The wave of grief as she is lifted into the hearse in front of me makes my stomach pitch and whirl. These emotions didn't hit me when my father passed. Then again, he was mostly absent as far as parenting goes during my childhood. Now, I'm in a position to gain half of his immense wealth. Losing the store is heavier than the possibility of being able to buy a franchise in every major city in the country. Unpacking my feelings is going to take time.

For the remainder of the service and reception, I feel like I'm walking through mud. Each conversation meant to add levity, anecdotes, and light around my boss doesn't hit the mark. They mean well but clearly knew Anne less than I did. She didn't shine in every room, nor did she befriend every customer. Anne hid in her office while I did those things. For her to receive my credit is disheartening. The truth is, nearly half the mourners inquire about the store's future. I smile, grit my teeth, and thank those paying their respects without providing answers. I don't have them.

Once the last guest leaves, I sign for the catering, and Ashton escorts me to my car.

"How are you doing?" he asks after kissing the back of my hand.

"Not sure. Why do I care so much? Anne was cold, distant, and barely civil to me."

"You love Seaside. You're scared what might happen to it. Your feelings are legitimate. You mentioned she was a single. Does she have any other family?"

I shake my head. "Not that I'm aware of."

"Maybe you should ask the long-time regulars. They may have more information than you," he suggests.

"It's a good idea. Just not today."

Ashton kisses my temple. "Are you up to driving?"

I nod. We grab his car, and he follows me home. I strip off my peacoat and black suit and tug on sweats. I burrow into the warmth of Ashton and the clothes. At some point, I fall asleep and wake up alone. Initially, my anger is front and center. Then I remember he has Penny. I grab my phone and find a text.

Ashton: Had to let Penny out. I'll be back with breakfast. xoxo

I don't answer, pad to my bed, and go back to sleep. Perhaps some rest will help me deal with the chaos surrounding Seaside and if I'm going to lose the only place I ever felt like I mattered, business-wise anyway. Personally, Ashton is a gift I want to keep.

CHAPTER TWELVE

ASHTON

The last time I met the family of someone I dated was in college. It took me three minutes in their home to realize they wanted a step up in status. The questions weren't about my affinity for their daughter but about the projected earnings of my family brand and my five-year plan. This was before my drink was poured.

Having briefly met Sera's brother, I'm cautiously optimistic about this holiday meal. Lex was gracious and didn't go overprotective big brother on me. It's clear he believes Sera's judgment is sound.

Me: Should I put Penny in her crate?

Her answer is instant. *Sera: Bring her. She'll occupy the kids. Plus, this is an all-day affair.*

Me: Okay. I'm grateful she can't hear hesitance in my response. With her leash and some treats, we pick up Sera.

She greets me with a bone-deep kiss that nearly knocks me off my feet.

"Morning, sweetheart."

She smiles, then she pets my dog. "Hi."

"You're in a good mood. What brought this on? I assume nothing has changed."

"I accepted a few facts. I can't control what happens with Seaside. Would I like it to be mine? Yes. Am I willing to buy it from her estate? Absolutely.

The next time I see the people who knew her the longest, I'll ask better questions."

"Proud of you."

"Thanks. It was your idea after all."

I open the passenger door. Penny hops up and sits on the center console until Sera is settled. Then my dog snuggles my woman. To say I'm jealous would be an understatement.

"Can you remind me of your sisters' names and the kids?"

She smirks at me. "Lex is married to Keeley. They don't have kids yet. Ellery is in the midst of a contentious divorce. Her children are Weston, who is twelve, and Cora is ten. She is the CFO at Celt with my brother. You met Sky and Lia. She works in HR at Celt. She doesn't love it but needed a distraction after she lost her husband. Then me."

"Best of the bunch in my humble opinion."

She laughs. "You haven't met them yet."

"Won't change how I feel about you." I wink at her and urge her to continue, "You have a younger sister, right?"

"Waverly is finishing her master's degree in public policy this spring at Georgetown."

"That's interesting. You would think business degrees would be required for each of you."

Sera freezes at my last statement.

Damn! I overstepped. "I'm sorry."

She takes my hand in hers. "You aren't wrong exactly. You heard my mother mention two affairs."

I acknowledge her statement.

"Well, Elle, Sky, and Wave aren't full siblings. While Lex and I don't care a bit, our father did."

"That is why he needs to have a son?"

"Yes. Lex doesn't agree with our father's position regarding male-only succession."

"That's archaic." The statement tumbles from my lips before I can stop it. I mean it, but blurting my thoughts probably isn't the best.

She shrugs. "Glad you agree. We'll figure it out. It's going to take some time."

I turn down a private road. "Are we in the right place?"

Sera giggles. "Yeah, Elle likes her privacy."

A massive mansion appears in the distance. It's quiet and peaceful when we exit the car. The leaves rustle on the slight breeze. The front door swings open before my woman is on her feet.

A young girl rushes toward us. "Hi." Penny jumps out and forgets her manners entirely as she bounces happily at Cora's feet.

Cora is grinning and excitedly petting my dog.

"Hey, sweetie. That's Penny. This is Ashton." Sera introduces us.

"He's cute, Auntie."

My face heats at the compliment. It eases my nerves as well. My goal today is to meet her family and make a good impression.

Sera shields her face as if I can't hear her and says, "I think so too."

I'm confident my girlfriend's opinion of me is greater than cute, but now isn't the time to discuss it further.

Penny dutifully follows Cora to the house. Why does my dog flock to Soren women? To be honest, I'm grateful. Penny brought Sera and I together.

Once we enter the house, my meet and greets pick up quickly with Cora as my guide. As we walk, she points out the people.

"This is Aunt Keeley. She makes the best pastries I've ever tasted."

Keeley raises her hand in a wave.

"She's right. Your croissants are delicious."

"Thank you." I don't miss the look that passes between Sera and her sister-in-law. It screams agreement with Cora's statement upon our arrival.

We enter a huge, modern living room.

"That's my brother, Weston, and our cousin, Lia."

"I 'member you. You have a puppy!" The sweet little girl with the cherub-like face smiles.

I crouch and raise my hand for a high five. "Nice to see you again. It appears your aunt might like me a little bit. That's Penny."

Lia giggles and pets my dog. Weston steps forward as if it's his turn to check me out.

I go with a fist bump for the preteen. "Hello."

"Did you already meet Uncle Lex?"

I frown. "Briefly, why?"

He nods. "Perfect. I don't have to ask any probing questions on Aunt Sera's behalf."

"As the only other guy in the family for now?" I inquire.

"Exactly," Weston replies and exits the conversation.

Sera leans closer. Her breath on my earlobe makes my brain spin with possibilities. "Sorry about him."

"No problem. It's his parents divorcing, right?"

Sera drops her head in acknowledgment.

I whisper, "It makes sense he's stepping up to a protector role for his family."

In my mind, I parse the list of her remaining siblings. There's Elle and Waverly left. True, I haven't seen Sky yet today, but we met already. Cora, with a fluffy escort, ushers us into the kitchen.

"Mom, Aunt Sera's here with a guy."

Ellery looks over her shoulder and smiles from near the sink. "Welcome. Please make yourself at home."

If Sera didn't share the information about her sisters, I would question the likelihood Waverly was related to her at all. She's a stunner with flowing auburn curls and piercing green eyes. She stands out from the rest of the Soren woman.

"Waverly, the youngest." She extends her hand to me.

"Ashton. Pleasure to meet you."

She smiles. "Has anyone interrogated you yet?"

Sera's hand tightens in mine.

"Only Sera."

"Well then. I'll stick to some basics. Okay with you?"

"Ask away."

Ellery shuts off the water and turns to face us.

Waverly's questions range from my profession to my siblings to whether I have an opinion on the best season of the year. It isn't until I've answered about ten questions does Lex join us in the kitchen,

"He's a good guy, ladies." Lex extends his hand to me.

"Happy Thanksgiving. Nice to see you again."

He grins at me. That brings the total of males in the house to three. "I'm going to need the name of your breeder. Keeley is hooked on Penny snuggles."

"Sure."

About twenty minutes after we arrive, the entire family gathers for a meal in the dining room. Ellery's home is made for large-scale parties. The pocket doors allow the table to extend into the formal living room. This is a feature my mother would appreciate. She always lamented about the inability to make the space meet her party needs. Our dinner parties were split into different rooms.

I was prepared for an inquisition, but aside from Waverly's inquiries, things are moving as if we're lifelong friends. We talk about football, the upcoming winter festival in town, and Penny stealing the hearts of the entire Soren clan.

Given the information I have about Sera's family, they are humble. Humble billionaires don't seem like a reasonable statement. Yet, they are. All of them. I see parallels between myself and my parents but not my brother. None of the Sorens are label hounds like Howie. Even more impressive is the kids aren't watching YouTube or playing games on a phone. They are coloring, reading, and chasing Penny around the house. I'm not a parent… yet, but I'm sure that's difficult.

Their demeanor shows through more when all the adults, except Ellery and Keeley, wash the dishes before dessert. I don't make a habit of looking for household staff. However, the lack of anyone was noticeable given the Soren family status. My mother hires help for holidays. I surmise that Keeley and Ellery prepared the meal, so they are exempt from dishes.

We clear the table, and Weston approaches me with a serious look on his face. Cora and Lia are beside him.

"Mr. Ashton, can we take Penny outside in the yard?"

"Is there a fenced area?"

Cora enthusiastically nods her head.

"Yes. Please stay in the fenced area."

The three kids hoot and holler before Lia responds, "You got it!"

"You made some friends for life bringing her with you today," Ellery states.

"If I left her, I would have to go home sooner. Sera indicated this was an all-day event, not a simple meal."

"She was correct. After dessert, we break out the cards."

"What do you play?"

Ellery winks. "Five-card stud. We don't use real money, and the kids play too."

I'm much less intimidated now.

After washing, we return to the dining room for dessert. Keeley has made a few trips with small plates and decadent-looking confections I'm dying to taste. I'm not an expert, but I see pumpkin pie, mini apple crumb bombs, a chocolate mousse, and a tart of unknown flavor. I need it all.

As the day passes, Sera relaxes as well.

"I told you it would be good."

She bestows a gorgeous smile on me. "I was worried about me, not you."

"Why?"

"I was terrified they would find something I missed."

I lean closer to Sera and kiss her cheek near her ear then whisper, "I'm an open book with you. You know more than anyone I dated before."

A cute smile curls at the corner of her mouth. "Same for me."

"We'll be fine."

"Until Saturday," she replies.

I shake my head. "My family and yours are similar. The only potential stumbling block is my brother. However, I don't think he's coming this weekend."

"Okay."

"My brother's opinion is inconsequential to me. We differ there."

Once everyone returns, including the kids and Penny, we pass the plates around the table and select our desserts.

"Is it horrible I want to try all of them?"

Sera laughs and the ribbon around my heart tightens. "No way. I am."

I glance over at Penny to find her sound asleep by the hearth in Cora's lap. It's adorable.

The Sorens show no mercy to me or the kids during poker after dinner. I do turn the tables for a few hands near the end though. Around eight, we say our goodbyes to her family. Sky and Lia are leaving as well. Lia and Sera are walking hand in hand to the SUV.

"I like him, Auntie."

Sera looks over at me and smirks. "Me too." Sera's family is important to her. I'm happy at least Lia likes me.

"Are we gonna keep him?"

My woman blushes, then answers, "Probably."

"Good." Lia throws her tiny arms around Sera as best she can and hugs tightly. "You next." I lower to her level, and she links her arms around my neck. "Be nice to Auntie. She's awesome."

After she releases me, I cross my heart. "I promise."

"Call me when you get home?" Sera asks her sister.

"Will do. Love you."

"Love you too."

This experience meeting my girlfriend's family was better than I hoped for. I'm confident the same will be true this weekend when I introduce Sera to mine.

CHAPTER THIRTEEN

SERAPHINA

Twisting to check the clock, I have thirty minutes before I need to get moving. Cozy in my bed with Ashton is worth cutting down my morning routine and skipping a workout. Approval from my siblings was appreciated. The last time a man met my family, it was a disaster. I'm pleased Ashton held his own. He kept every name straight and trounced Lex and Ellery in poker. I'm confident Penny wasn't the only reason the kids liked him as well.

I see more holidays with Ashton in the future. How will it work when he needs to go home? I'm not sure yet, especially since I have zero plans to leave Mystic Cove. My desire and intention to stay in my hometown could be a roadblock for our relationship. In this moment, being wrapped in his arms in the morning is heavenly, and I don't care one bit.

"You should stop thinking so deeply this early."

I twist to face him. "How do you know it's heavy?"

"You tensed. We can't have that, especially before the busiest day for the store even starts."

I frown. "You're coming with me?"

"Yup. I'm going to bring Penny home, freshen up, and spend time with you at the store."

"Did you mention this before? Do you normally take Black Friday off?"

"No. I was going to surprise you when I showed up. I spilled the beans a tad early. Normally, I'm off today. I set up my latest proposal to be delivered first thing too."

I pepper his face with kisses. "Yay! You can bring Penny. She's good with people. Plus, if it gets crazy, we can trap her in the rear hallway."

"Sounds perfect. We need to move though, don't we?"

"Yes, but I don't mind."

Now it's his turn to frown. "Because?"

"We'll be back later."

He chuckles, kisses the tip of my nose, and stands.

"I could bounce a quarter off your ass."

Ashton turns beet red.

"Don't get shy on me now."

"Not used to my woman being so… honestly vocal. I like it."

I tilt my head and add, "Good. Don't think I can change."

"You're perfect exactly as you are."

Warmth and giddiness wash over me. Where has he been hiding? A nagging little voice in my mind replies, *"New York."*

"Before I forget, I meant to ask last night, but we were otherwise engaged. Will you join me at the Celt Holiday Soirée?"

He raises an eyebrow. "Was that a complaint?"

Ashton and I between the sheets is unmatched. He's attentive, giving, and insatiable. "Never."

He grins at me. "Absolutely. Tuxedo?"

I nod.

"You in a sexy cocktail dress, I'm definitely in."

Just under an hour later, I pick up my order from the café and walk around the block to Seaside Books. This year, I didn't advertise our specials widely. Preparing for Anne's services, though it wasn't much for me to do and not knowing where I stand, hampered my efforts a bit. Yet, there's a line at the door when I arrive.

"Good morning, all. Give me one minute, and I'll be ready for you." I inhale deeply, flick the lights on throughout the store, and open for business.

The first wave of customers enter the store. Ashton and Penny arrive as the early morning patrons step inside. He took her for a walk while I grabbed our breakfast.

"How can I help?" he asks. I direct him to guide the customers as best he can because I haven't given him a tutorial on the cash register. I can't help but watch him. He's a natural with the customers, especially the kids. Penny certainly assists with her wet kisses and excited demeanor.

Before I know it, it's noon, and our breakfast is cold and uneaten. Inwardly, I frown because my caramel latté is as well. Iced coffee isn't my thing. The crowd has thinned, but there are still a few patrons milling around in the store.

"Can you go grab food for us from Keeley?"

Ashton checks our surroundings and kisses me. "I ordered lunch when I walked Penny about an hour ago. Keeley said she would send it over."

"You're pretty amazing."

"As are you."

Someone clears their throat.

I smile when I find Alma and Stan ready to check out.

"Mrs. Swanson, thank you for stopping by today."

"Of course, dear. Only place to buy books. Plus, the staff is gifted at what she does."

I catch myself shaking my head. "I love helping people find an escape into pages of adventure or fantasy."

"It's more that."

I scan her books, and she asks, "Have you read Anne's letter yet?"

I purse my lips and drop my head. Reading her final words to me could be the end of my life as I know it. I could lose this place where I'm most comfortable and happy.

Alma reaches out and takes my hand in hers. "While I don't know the contents of your letter, I assure you, Anne wouldn't be harsh. I urge you to open it, Sera. If nothing else, Anne would demand compliance."

I can't help but laugh heartily. "You're right. She would. Anne was nothing if not precise. Thank you for the nudge."

Mr. Swanson simply shakes his head. "Let's leave the young people to their customers, my dear." He offers his wife an arm, which she gratefully accepts. Stan is the sweetest doting husband. I want that level of devotion when I'm old and gray.

As they leave, Keeley arrives with more food than we could possibly need for one meal.

"You're a lifesaver," I state, digging into the bag unceremoniously.

She wrinkles her nose. "I think your praise should be for Ashton. All I did was deliver it before I go to my other location."

I look up at my sister-in-law and add, "Thank you."

"Don't forget about our appointment next weekend with Kelly." She reminds me.

Kelly owns a custom couture dress boutique in Maine. We have an appointment for our final fittings. Luckily, Kelly Barnett can craft elegant designs with a few ideas and measurements. She has never failed me.

"I won't forget. Is it too late to add a tuxedo for Ashton?" I love trying on her designs. They hit the mark. Every. Single. Time.

"No." Keeley turns her attention to him. "Please text Lex your measurements, and he'll get them to Kelly."

"Will do. Thanks again for the food."

"My pleasure." Keeley smiles and floats out of the store.

There's a short lull allowing us to eat the sandwiches and drink hot coffee.

"You still haven't opened it?"

My eyes flutter closed briefly. "I'm terrified. I could lose this place. If I hold out perhaps reality will stay the same."

"Or…."

I don't need him to finish his thought aloud nor do I complete it for him. I thread my fingers with his. "Will you sit with me when I read it?"

"Of course. Do you have it with you?"

I shake my head. It's behind my grandmother's jewelry box on my dresser. I didn't request family jewels or antiques. The intricate wooden keepsake holder was the only thing I wanted. Grandfather happily obliged.

It appears our reprieve is over. Patrons enter the store at a steady pace for the rest of the day. Penny is a welcome addition to the vibe. Parents shop while their kids pet her. Penny switches between groups with her tail wagging furiously. When I run the tally at the end of the day, I'm floored. The sales exceeded our highest day by twenty percent. I smile and hope Anne is proud despite our tense relationship.

The last customer is a young woman. She purchases a few books with stuffies for her niece. I escort her out and lock the front door behind her.

"How do you feel about comfort food for dinner?" Ashton asks.

"Sounds perfect, but…."

Ashton laughs. "I know you don't have food. I ordered groceries for delivery while I was at the cottage this morning. They should arrive at your place in thirty minutes."

"You're the best ever!" I kiss him. He's the first man I've dated who truly takes care of me. I could get used to it. The fact I like it shocks me a little. Once I realized that my father didn't want me because I was female and my mother didn't have a nurturing bone in her body, I relied mostly on myself and Lex with guidance from Walter and Cara. My relationships with my sisters are great. Little did Lex and I know that our bond was stronger for other reasons.

"Only for you. Let's go."

As expected, the food arrives on time. While I put things away, Ashton warms gourmet tomato soup—his words—and prepares grilled cheese on sourdough. He wasn't wrong about the comfort part. These are delicious.

"You're holding out on your cooking abilities?"

"Not at all. The occasion and weather didn't present themselves until today."

"Good point." When we finish, I burrow into his side as best I can. He willingly allows me to invade his personal space anytime I choose. My mind spins with what Anne could've possibly written to me. Maybe she was aware about my family wealth. Honestly, I'm not sure.

"Seraphina." My name never sounded so heavenly until him.

I lift my gaze to meet his.

"I will hold you as long as you like, but you should open the letter."

"Promise?"

"Yes."

I stretch and kiss his soft lips before pushing off his chest to my feet. "I'll be right back."

I take a deep breath and retrieve Anne's last words to me. Retaking my seat beside him, I slip my finger beneath the heavy ivory flap. Even in death, Anne had style and grace. The letter is sealed by a wax stamp with her initials. It's beautiful, and I don't want to break it. However, I need to find out what she wanted to say but couldn't or didn't when she was alive.

Seraphina,

When you showed up for your interview, I wasn't sure what to do. You were overqualified and certainly deserved a higher salary for your skill set. I sincerely apologize for failing to open up to you and not sharing my connection to your family. Your grandmother Collette and I were close friends. It was certainly before you were born. Your grandfather and my fiancé served together in the military. She and I met at a family readiness group and hit it off. We spent a lot of time together while our guys were overseas. Collette was the only person aside from Alma who knew about my engagement to Peter. We decided to wait to marry upon his return rather than rush to the altar like so many others did. Perhaps had I pushed, I would've had the pleasure of being Mrs. Peter Collins for a brief moment rather than not at all.

All that is to say, you impressed me day after day. Your work ethic is impeccable despite your family wealth. You made my little escape from the world bloom into a profitable business while showcasing local authors and viewpoints. Some would believe a woman like you doesn't need Seaside Books. My opinion is quite the opposite. You belong at the helm. No one deserves it more.

I inhale deeply and swipe the tears from my cheeks. She was friendly with my grandmother. I'm shocked.

"Is it sad?" Ashton whispers as if the same question at a normal volume could mean something else.

Shaking my head is all I can muster. I exhale and continue reading.

In the office safe, you'll find my estate plan. The combination is your birthday. Please deliver it to the attorney of your choice so the corporation and my other holdings can be transferred to you.

You are the daughter I dreamed of having with Peter. I'm proud of you and your accomplishments, especially when your parents failed to share the same sentiment. I can't thank you enough for making my dream flourish. Please continue the legacy for yourself and your future family.

With love,

Anne

The emotions welling within me are hard to contain. As if he knows what the letter contains or how I might react, Ashton tightens his hold on me.

"She left me… everything. I thought she tolerated me," I manage to share. Tears prick my eyes, and my throat is tight and dry.

"That's amazing. You get to run the store as you see fit."

"I was but didn't feel appreciated until it was…."

"Too late," he suggests.

I nod.

Ashton kisses my temple. "Clearly, she was aware of how much you loved Seaside."

"I wish she talked to me more while she was here." I'm a mess. My heart is heavy and full at once. It's an odd mixture of feelings. On one hand, I'm sad she's gone. On the other, I'm overjoyed that Seaside is mine.

"We should get some sleep."

"Will you stay?" The words tumble from my lips before I can stop them. He doesn't officially work on the weekends.

"Yes. I'll take Penny for a quick walk." He wakes his sleepy pup. She lopes to the stairs, then they disappear behind the door.

I am the owner of Seaside. I was fully prepared to purchase it from Anne. My mind is spinning with ideas about what to change or add. I would like to add a coffee bar. One sponsored by the Keeley's café makes the most sense. If only there was a way to connect the two buildings. That is a pie-in-the-sky notion but not a horrible one. There's only one structure between us.

Before I get too deep into my thoughts, I schedule a text to my brother and clear our dishes. By the time Ashton and Penny return, everything is drying, and we turn in for the night. I mentally run through my day tomorrow. Work will be great. I'm nervous to meet his parents though. It's telling I never have been with any other man.

CHAPTER FOURTEEN

ASHTON

I'm ecstatic for Sera. She'll be able to run the store her way. Then again, I gather she has been all along except Anne didn't share praise or kudos.

After breakfast and despite the cold, we walk to Seaside this morning. Like yesterday, there's a line at the front door when we arrive.

"Perhaps I should expand the hours?"

I blurt without much thought, "I would suggest looking at the books first."

She grins and kisses my cheek. "Good point." With the store lights warming up, Sera admits the first customers of the day. I guide a few people to the correct sections and speak eloquently on a few newer releases I happen to have read. Penny is a huge hit with the kids. The tiny redhead with ringlet curls is sitting still with Penny's head in her lap. The grin on her face is infectious. She's absorbing pets and cuddles in the kids' reading area while their parents shop.

"I might need a Penny for myself," she whispers as she passes by me midmorning, "Read to a puppy is a great idea."

"It is." One of her Christmas gifts just became simple.

The patrons flow in steadily. We don't stop for lunch. Near three, there's a lull. The only guest in the store has already checked out. Their son is reluctantly saying goodbye to my dog.

"Can you handle out here for a few? I need to pull the documents from the safe and check my messages."

"Up for it alone?"

Sera smiles, and my heart pounds. That joy drew me to her. She moves closer and says, "It'll be weird, but yes. Thank you for knowing it will be difficult." With a light kiss, she turns and walks confidently down the narrow hallway to the office.

I notice that it's been nearly an hour since Sera went to the office. I call Penny and search for her at the end of the dimly lit hall.

She's a vision behind that desk. The concentration on her face is mesmerizing.

I tap the doorframe with my knuckles to avoid startling her. I fail.

She inhales sharply. "Hey."

"You okay?"

"I think so. Have I been long?" Then she glances at the antique clock on the credenza. "I'm sorry."

"No problem at all. We have it covered." Penny casually walks around the desk and climbs onto Sera's lap.

Sera points to an elegant bound book on the desk. "She kept a journal of every idea and notion, crazy or not, I came up with over the years. I never felt seen by her until right now."

"Sometimes we have difficulty expressing ourselves face-to-face. Anne loved you. Her way of showing it was to give you the product of your hard work."

Sera rises from the chair and throws her arms around me. "Thank you. She gave me more than the store. When Anne said everything, she meant it. This expandable folder contains her estate plan documents as well as directions to her home, alarm system access, and keys as well as contact information for her gardener."

The door chime sounds. "Pack that up. It's nearly time to leave for dinner."

I rush to the front and greet the young couple. They are very precise with their shopping plan and the titles they desire. Within fifteen minutes, loaded down with their books, they leave. In the meantime, Sera has emerged with Penny prancing beside her.

At six, we exit the store and hurry to her loft. I have never seen a woman transform so quickly. She chose a green sheath dress with a matching jacket. Her hair is pinned half up, and curls bounce around her face, and she freshened her makeup. Then again, Sera is stunning daily. While she dressed, I changed into a suit and tie for dinner.

"You look beautiful."

"You clean up well yourself."

"Wait till you see me in a custom tuxedo."

She smiles, which was what I am aiming for. Sera takes my arm, and we hurry to meet my parents.

"How nervous should I be right now?"

Minutes later, I pull into the valet of the club. It's private. Ideally, the photos won't be plastered in the papers prematurely announcing an engagement. It would force a conversation, but I'm not ready to be engaged to the woman I'm falling for hard. Especially not before I share my feelings with her.

My parents arrived before us. The maître d' escorts us to join them. I reach out to shake my father's hand, but we hug instead. It's unusual but not unheard of. I follow suit with my mother and introduce my gorgeous girlfriend.

"Please meet Sera."

She extends her hand. My father takes it, but my mother hugs her as if we've been dating for years.

Sally Calloway, clad in a navy pantsuit states, "It's a pleasure."

Gracious as ever, Sera replies, "You as well. Thank you for traveling. I appreciate the accommodation."

"You're welcome," my mother answers.

I hear a ruckus near the entrance. I know that voice. Ire rises from my belly. He always messes everything up. Did I meet Sera because he's a fuck up? Yes. Will I give him credit? Hell no.

"My family is already seated. You can't prevent me from joining them."

Damn it! "Did you invite Howie?" I mutter under my breath.

"No." My father adamantly answers.

I tilt my head. "Well, he's here and making a scene." Leaning closer to Sera, I say, "I'll be back."

My father and I make our way to the lobby.

"He's denying me entry." Howie, who looks disheveled and possibly drunk, points a finger at the host.

"What are you doing here?" I ask.

"I came to meet the next Mrs. Calloway," Howie answers slowly. "Will she take your name? Maybe you're the gold digger in this relationship."

Confession time. I called his ex-wife that once. I wasn't wrong, but I still shouldn't have said it.

"How did you know about dinner?" My tone is calm. It's completely opposite of my emotional state, which is ready to erupt. He has messed with my livelihood and now with my relationship.

"Mom mentioned it when we spoke a few days ago."

Inwardly, I grumble.

While I talk with Howie, I use the term loosely, my father has smoothed things over with the club manager.

"Ashton, please go back to our table. Howard, follow me," our father demands.

The staff is placing another chair at the table. Sera and my mother are having a lighthearted conversation as I join them again.

I thread my fingers through Sera's beneath the table. Given her contentious relationship with her mother, she knows support is needed.

"What can I do?" she offers.

Leaning close, I murmur, "You're already doing plenty."

About five minutes later, my father and brother join us at our table. I intend to forego the niceties of introducing Sera. My father does it briefly on my behalf. Rather than a joyful first meeting with my girlfriend, dinner turns into a nearly silent meal complete with glaring looks from my brother across the table. Maintaining my composure is only possible because of Sera's death grip on my hand. It reminds me of where we are, why we are here, and how making a scene of my own won't get me what I want. There's no going back to the introductory dinner I hoped for at this point.

Our server rightfully picked up on the tension and proceeds expeditiously. I'm appreciative of his efforts.

Soon after our entrees are delivered, Howie addresses Sera. "What do you do for a living?"

"I run a bookstore," she answers.

Her answer isn't the complete truth. I understand and support her hedged response. She is the owner now, though not officially.

"Isn't that beneath a woman of your stature?" Howie asks.

Sera is stunned silent at his statement.

My brother just showed her how different siblings can be with his rude and callous statement.

"Don't answer him. We're leaving." I throw my napkin on the table and stand. I turn my gaze toward my brother. "You can't come here, uninvited I might add, and insult Sera because you failed at life and love."

I pull out her chair.

"It was a pleasure meeting you," she states to my parents before we exit the restaurant quickly but politely.

While we wait at the valet, I take her hands in mine. "I'm so sorry about him."

"It's not your fault," Sera replies. "My skin isn't as thick as Lex's. He's better at handling people like Howie who insinuate things because they don't want light shining on them."

This woman is perfect. She could run for the hills, but she's firmly beside me. "Thank you."

"I don't quit when life gets are hard or uncomfortable."

I kiss her temple. "Thank you. I'm grateful."

The valet arrives with my SUV.

As I accept my keys, my father calls out to me. "Ashton, wait."

My mother keeps stride with him making their way to us.

Rather than address me, he speaks directly to Sera. "It was lovely meeting you. I hope Howard's rudeness doesn't impact future meals."

Sera tightens her fingers in mine and smiles. "It won't."

"Lovely," my mother adds. She leans closer and whispers, presumably so Sera doesn't hear her. "Hold onto her. She's good for you."

"I plan to." I reply in equal volume, although I'm confident our exchange was overheard. I glance up to the doorway and see Howard approaching. Cupping Sera's arm, I escort her hastily into my vehicle. I cross my arms over my chest and wait for him. Frankly, I don't want him to follow me to the cottage or Sera's. If he knew about our dinner, he likely is aware of the address of my rental at least.

"You think you're better than me." He throws the accusation like I should be insulted by the words.

"I'm not doing this with you. You made your choices, which are vastly different from mine. It isn't my fault the results weren't what you hoped for."

Howie steps up to me, and we're nose to nose. "You're an asshole. You took my job!"

I step back and shake my head. "No. You forfeited your job when you failed to meet the requirements. I'm trying to save the company."

My brother grits his teeth, draws his arm back, and punches me in the mouth. My jaw aches immediately as my teeth crunched together from the force of his fist.

Our mother shouts, "Howard!"

My father steps between us, preventing me from laying my brother out on the ground. Would I have retaliated? Unlikely. I have a sense of decorum as opposed to my brother. The altercation was caught on camera as well as the aftermath, which will add additional duties to smooth over.

Sera throws open the door and rushes around the car to my side. She slides her hands on both sides of my face and turns me away from my family.

"I'm okay." My assurance isn't well received.

She purses her lips as if she's holding back her words and emotions. Sera guides me to the passenger side of the car. "Get in."

I bring my rapidly swelling mouth near her ear. "I like you bossy."

Her eyes flutter closed, and she tilts her head, requesting compliance with her demand.

I do as she requested. Sera skirts around the hood, sits in the driver's seat, and pulls away.

"There are not enough ways for me to apologize." I mutter through the pain. It's bearable but unpleasant.

Initially, Sera doesn't respond. She's focused on the road or keeping her emotions in check. I'm not sure which. Sera pulls into the driveway of the cottage and kills the engine.

"Come on. You need ice."

Her demeanor is a bit standoffish yet caring. It's confusing. I'm not sure what to make of it.

Once inside, she opens the freezer and prepares an ice pack for my jaw.

"Please say something," I plead with her.

She sighs heavily and sits beside me on the cushy couch. "I don't have anything to add. I'm not angry with you. I'm disappointed your brother ruined our meal."

"You're a better person than I am. While I wouldn't in general, I wanted to pound my brother into the pavement."

"Because?"

"To show I could despite being younger and to express my displeasure with him disrespecting you and our dinner." A mixture of emotions vie for supremacy. "Aside from our vastly differing opinions on how to spend our family wealth, Howie doesn't understand how to keep the company moving forward for future generations, including his daughter."

"That's why Mitchell put you in charge of both sides of the business?"

"Yes. It's a lot for one person, but my portfolio mostly runs itself. I have a set schedule of check-ins and visits."

"Will your father fire him now?"

I shrug. "That would make sense businesswise but due to optics, probably not."

"I get it," she replies.

No woman I've ever dated "got it." Even my ex from college whose parents were wealthy but to a lesser degree didn't understand the pressures of having filthy rich parents. Sera does.

I pull the ice pack from my jaw and kiss her tenderly. Instead of spending the rest of my holiday weekend relaxing, I'm going to be dealing with my brother's behavior and likely rumors of an engagement to Sera. While I can see us together in the future, it's too soon to be thinking about marriage. Right?

There is no defined timeline to know if someone is your person, and Seraphina Soren is mine without question.

CHAPTER FIFTEEN

SERAPHINA

Despite the end of our dinner, it went well otherwise. While Ashton and Mitchell were dealing with Howie's arrival, my chat with Sally was nice and cordial. We chatted about my education and the store mostly. She never once asked about the headlines or whether I truly was an heiress. Yes, but how many billions is the question.

To be honest, having hundreds of billions terrifies me. I intend to be like Lex. He's had access to his initial trust for about eight years. Overall, my brother has made it grow and not spent huge sums until recently. Purchasing two homes in two states can make a dent. Except he has probably already replaced the asset purchases with his dividends. Until learning about Anne's estate, that would be my position upon my birthday in a few months. Now, things are a little more complicated.

Ashton is sound asleep in the bedroom. I open the door to the backyard and let Penny out. I watch her just in case she's crafty near the gate. With coffee for us, I return quietly.

"Morning," he grumbles.

"Hi. How's your face?"

He attempts to smile and winces. Then he frowns.

"Still hot, if you ask me."

"Much appreciated. Did you have plans today?"

"I should air out Anne's house—my house and clean the fridge." A weird and eerie sense passes over me, I have no idea what that means. Is it a charming little cottage or a massive colonial? I would lean toward the former. What is her decorating style? If Seaside is any indication, minimalist would be my guess.

"Are you going to keep it?"

I shake my head. "I don't know. I've never been there and I'm intrigued. I'm hanging on for the surprise."

"Want company?" he offers.

"Yes. I need to get fresh clothes first."

The relief on his face is palpable. Spending the day with me will push off dealing with Howie. I don't mind one bit. He gulps down his coffee. "Give me fifteen minutes." Then he hurries into the bathroom.

As promised, he's ready to go. I make quick work of getting ready when we arrive at my loft. Without checking first, I input the address, and Ashton follows the prompts. My gut churns the closer we get to Anne's... home.

I realize as we near the end of the trip, we are close to Lex and Keeley's. Without a thought, I text my brother.

Me: You home?

Lex: Yeah, why?

Me: It appears Anne was your neighbor. We're parking in the driveway diagonally from you.

Lex: Can we come by?

Me: Yes.

"Is this what you expected?"

"No, I pictured a tiny English cottage. This is... Lex and Keeley are on their way. They live across the street." A small house on the water would be more my speed. From the outside, this house is spectacular. The landscaping is pristine, and the water views are beautiful. The garden is magnificent. I wonder how many acres there are?

Lex and Keeley join us. We greet each other.

"Ready for this?"

"Good or bad for the chances of keeping it?"

"Definitely the former, though I love my loft." As much as it suits me, the huge modern colonial is near my brother and his soon-to-be-growing family. Keeley is going to have a baby mid-next year. Unfortunately—only to get our mother off his back—it's a girl.

I pluck the key from my purse and enter. Aside from an expected staleness, I'm floored. The home has a two-story foyer and a grand staircase. Each room is perfectly appointed. There's an office on the main floor, which is decorated as a bedroom. I suppose Anne was remaining on the first level. I nearly burst into tears when I slide the pocket door to the right, revealing a library with books from floor to ceiling.

"Are you sure she didn't reach into your head and build this place for you?" Lex asks.

My brother isn't wrong. "No way she could know." I ponder his question more and wonder if I ever mentioned my desire to have an actual library in my home. I don't recall. However, it means Anne and I were more alike than I thought. That notion brings up mixed feelings for me.

As I walk back to the stairs, Ashton's phone rings. Instantly, he scowls.

"Your Dad?"

He drops his head.

"Go, it's fine."

He kisses my cheek and wanders toward the formal sitting room.

"That about the fight with his brother?" Keeley asks.

I purse my lips and reply, "Yeah. How bad are the photos?"

Keeley smiles. "You look amazing."

Damn it! "And the headline?"

She sets her hand on my forearm. "Speedy Nuptials Planned for Calloway Heir."

"Yikes!"

"Well?" Keeley grins.

We're standing in the upstairs hallway at this point. I look behind us and note Lex isn't there. Not that I don't share with him, but this falls more into my sister-in-law's wheelhouse for now. "I wouldn't say no to a ring, but we would be engaged for a while."

Keeley hops up and down. "I'm so happy for you."

"Thanks. Now, I have a stunning home, the store, and the trust to handle."

"You've got this!" We loop arms and walk to the master suite.

The master suite looks like a luxury hotel room complete with a fireplace, sitting area, and a covered balcony with water views. It's gorgeous. Mine. I still can't wrap my head around the fact this place belongs to me. I tour the remaining bedrooms upstairs—four of them—with Keeley. Lex also took a call and remained in the kitchen. When we make our way back to our guys, their mood has shifted significantly.

I hear Lex shouting in the kitchen, which isn't normal. Ashton is sitting on the couch in the formal living room with his head in his hands.

"I'll check on Lex," Keeley says before striding toward her husband.

Silently, I take a seat next to Ashton on the couch. Frustration and anger are rolling off him in waves. For a solid five minutes, he says nothing. I sit beside him with our hands linked, wondering how bad the reaction is from the fight.

"My father is making me go back to New York," he finally mumbles softly.

My heart sinks. "When?" So much for that ring.

"Tonight."

I manage to prevent my voice from cracking by the slightest margin when I ask, "Why?"

"He told me to stop doing Howie's job. He's considering liquidating the company."

"Do you get a vote?" I ask. We've talked about his job but not if he wanted to run the company long term after bailing out his brother.

"Whether or not to sell? No, I don't." Dejected is the best way I can describe his tone and demeanor. I don't blame him. He's been working for the company for years. Ashton fully expected to take over soon after fixing his brother's failure. A serious expression meets mine. "I don't want to break up, but long distance isn't going to be easy."

"Neither do I, but you're right. I can't leave now."

Ashton leans forward and kisses my forehead. "I know. I wouldn't ask you to either despite how much I would prefer to wake up with you daily."

"Are you still willing to come to the soirée, or should I cancel your tuxedo?"

Immediately, he shakes his head. "I'll be here late every Friday until decisions are made."

A tear rolls down my cheek. "Really?"

"Absolutely. This is a delay, not an end. You are my person. Now, we need to figure out how to make it work."

Relief and a bit of anger ripple through me. Not at Ashton but toward Mitchell. From the outside, it looks as if my boyfriend and his job are going to pay the price for his older brother's stupidity. We're going to be apart sooner than initially anticipated at the very least.

Part of me knew my relationship was too good to be true. Not Ashton himself, but the distance between our homes should've given me pause. Despite this issue, I'm glad I agreed to coffee.

"I'm sorry, but I have to go home. Would you prefer I call an Uber?"

I shake my head. "Only if you want to pack up alone."

"I'll savor every minute you're willing to give me," Ashton replies.

I kiss him and add, "I'll be right back." Joining Lex and Keeley in the kitchen, I find he's done with the call.

"Mom or something else?"

"A work emergency not related to our mother. One of our ships has been boarded by pirates."

"How? We adjust our routes and avoid hot spots, if you will."

"It appears the captain's family was abducted, and the ship was the ransom," Lex answers. The weight of this issue is heavy on his shoulders. "You don't look happy anymore either?"

"I'm not. I have to get going. Can you lock up?"

Keeley shakes her head. "We can leave as well. Need to talk?"

I shake my head. "Not now. Ashton has been summoned home tonight."

My sister-in-law hugs me and whispers, "I'm sorry, sweets."

"Me too. We'll figure it out."

The three of us walk toward the main foyer, and Ashton joins us. "It was a pleasure seeing you again." The guys bro hug, and he hugs Keeley.

"You as well," Lex offers, and we exit the double door in the front.

"Want a ride?" I ask them.

Lex smiles and threads his fingers through Keeley's. "No, we're good. Love you."

"Love you," I reply.

The remaining time I spend with Ashton is solemn and all too short. Once we arrive at the cottage, he makes quick work of packing his things. Penny is none the wiser, running around in circles in the fenced area. Needing to do something, I put Penny's bowls and food into a reusable bag. Then I cull through the items in the refrigerator and put them in an insulated one.

"Thank you. You didn't have to."

I shrug and close the now empty appliance. Random dressings and sauces fill half the garbage pail. We make a trip to his car and the trash container outside. Once more and his personal items are loaded up. Keeping my emotions in check is difficult. I'm angry and sad. Sharing that won't get us anywhere though. More importantly, it isn't his fault or his choice.

"I'll call you when I get home." His last word hit harder than I anticipated. He never called Mystic Cove home. I was hoping we had a few more months to figure our relationship out before he had to leave. Secretly, I wanted him to stay. I believed Ashton when he indicated this was a bump in the road, but my past makes me skeptical.

He draws me into his arms and kisses me deeply. Internally, I struggle not to push him against the wall and convince him not to leave. This isn't his choice, and I need to remember that.

The heat from our kiss winds from my lips to my toes and swirls around my heart. I resist my urge to steal an hour in the bedroom though it's difficult.

"Drive safely. Talk later." I kiss him lightly and reach down to pet Penny.

Ashton opens the door, and his matchmaking furball hops into the passenger seat. He looks back at me twice before closing the door behind him and pulling away.

After a few minutes pass, I drive to my loft and wallow in a pint of ice cream from the shop near Seaside before curling into my bed... alone.

CHAPTER SIXTEEN

ASHTON

My apartment is stale, like Sera's new house. She worked her ass off for Anne and was handsomely rewarded. The sheer fact that she expected nothing from her former boss made the recognition of the same even sweeter. Anger and sadness vied for attention during the nearly four-hour ride home with endless traffic jams and two pit stops for Penny. We were just getting started—a fact my father was aware of. Hell, introducing them to Sera was huge for me. They haven't met anyone since college. Making career choices wasn't in my playbook for this year or even next as far as starting over anyway. Until this ride along Interstate 95, I hadn't considered working somewhere other than Calloway Investments.

If I'm not tied to my family business, I can't fathom the myriad of options available to me just yet. Don't want to, but it may be necessary. I haul my luggage inside, empty the food, and set up Penny's bowls.

The rest can wait. I plop onto my couch and call Sera.

"Hey," she answers nearly immediately.

"Hi."

We chitchat about the traffic and then silence exists between us for nearly a minute.

"I'm...."

"Not your fault."

I inhale sharply and end the silent stewing on both ends. "I'll call you tomorrow."

"Good night, Ashton."

Hanging up feels heavy. I refuse to let this woman slip away because of my lazy brother.

First thing the next morning, I follow my old routine and clock in before most people wake up.

My first call is a follow-up on the proposal I sent last week.

The boutique owner is gracious. "We received a similar offer a few days prior to yours. We went with that one because the terms were better for us."

I frown. The work I've been doing in the last few months has been summarily thwarted. How? Two rejections out of two, it's unheard of. "Would you be willing to share the name of the investment company who outbid me, if you will?"

"HCNC Investments."

"Thank you for your time. Good luck with your expansion."

I end the call and rehash my approach to the owners of the jewelry store and the boutique. I didn't change anything. My presentation and profit margin for Calloway was similar to those in the past.

Before I start researching, my father appears in the doorway of my office.

"You're here." His tone seems surprised.

"You summoned me." I attempt to keep the disdain in my tone at a minimum. I'm marginally successful as my father doesn't scowl at me. "Is there any wiggle room in your mind about selling?"

"Some, but not much. Why do you ask?"

I frown. "My latest offers were rejected. It doesn't make sense. I would like some time to investigate the company or companies that beat me out."

"My plan is to find a suitable buyer within the next six months. I doubt your research will garner evidence for me to change my position, but you have at least until an offer sheet is signed."

"Thank you. Does the sale include a position for me or not?" I bottle my anger as best I can. Exploding on my father won't do any good. I have only ever worked for Calloway. If I knew this would be the outcome, I might have chosen a different path. Which one? I have no idea because it was never an option. A few months ago, I was sold on the opportunity of running Calloway Investments on my own. Now, it isn't the plan anymore.

"Not necessarily. I have plenty of connections to find you a suitable job." My father answers.

"I can run Calloway. I'll hire a capable second," I state without thinking it through.

"If you and Howie aren't in it together, I'm selling."

While I should keep this thought to myself, I ask, "Why should I suffer because Howie can't manage his life?"

"The company is family owned and operated. It's how I formed it and wanted it to stay. I agree, you're getting screwed by a liquidation as far as a job is concerned. However, look at it as a chance to figure out what you want to do with your future instead of doing what I told you to do."

For the first time, my father bears some responsibility for pigeonholing me in my profession. "I don't like it, but I understand your position."

"For the company or for Sera?"

"Both. Running Calloway has always been the end goal for me. You're changing the rules."

"Ash—"

"I'm disappointed. My relationship with Sera didn't have to factor into my profession until today." I didn't have a girlfriend with wife-potential before now.

He nods and leaves without adding more. On top of figuring out who backs HCNC, I need to search for a job commensurate with my skill set. While I like working for the family business, I don't have to as far as money is concerned. What would I choose if I could pick anything at all? Honestly, I don't know. I never had to consider my professional aspirations before.

The rest of the day, I check in on my clients and manage the public relations fallout from the photo and article with the consultant my father hired. I also send a message to the custom jewelry store owner to see if she will divulge the name of her investor.

Finally, as I'm ready to leave the office for the day, I check my messages.

Sera: Thank you. The flowers are gorgeous!

Me: You're welcome. I would've preferred to deliver them myself.

Me: Sorry it took so long to answer.

Sera: Me too. No problem. I'll call you later. Xoxo

Me: xoxo

I stare at the characters in the text, wishing I could actually hug and kiss Sera later. Reminded that I have four more days to go before I can hold my woman, I pack up and return home to my other woman. The only other kind allowed in my opinion. I'm sure Sera's too.

Penny and I take a long walk despite the chill in the air before I make dinner. After eating, I sit in the side chair facing toward the shore. My view is decent in the spring and summer. At this time of the year, the holiday lights across the river are plentiful.

Near seven, my phone chimes. My body warms at the thought it could be Sera. My temperature plummets when I see my brother's name on the screen. To avoid him calling incessantly or showing up, I answer.

"Hello, Howie. What do you want?"

"Can you give me Sera's phone number? Dad is demanding a personal apology."

Absolutely not! I reel in my anger and quickly come up with a solution that will work for me. The last thing I want is for him to have a direct line to contact Sera. "Not now. I want to speak with her first."

"That's fair. Thank you. Shoot me a text when you have an answer."

Then the line goes dead. Weird. Sera deserves an apology, but I don't? I'm not evolved enough to let a sucker punch roll off my back even from my brother. Before I redial Howie to give him a piece of my mind, a video call request from Sera illuminates my phone. I happily accept.

"Hi, sweetheart," I answer. Her beautiful face fills my screen.

Her head tilts to the side as she greets me. "Hi. Are you okay?"

"Yes. No. Yes." Sera waits for me to continue. We may be apart right now, but in the time we spent together, we learned a fair amount about each other. She knows I'm careful with my word choice. "Howie asked for your number to apologize. I wanted to get permission from you first."

"What about you? You deserve one as well."

She sees me. "It wasn't offered."

"That's bullshit! He showed up unannounced. He ruined our meal. Howie made a scene and then he hit you!"

The fire in her words and expression make me smile. Not because she is angry. She has every right to be for herself. Sera is more pissed on my behalf. "Easy tiger! I know better than to expect the right thing from my brother as it pertains to sibling norms." He's older. Howie doesn't believe one is necessary because I'm—was—working both his job and mine. "I am owed an apology, but I will never get it. I've accepted that fact."

She relaxes slightly.

I add, "I truly appreciate your intention to throw down on my behalf. I love your feistiness. Howie doesn't deserve the energy. As far as him contacting you, what about I call him and conference you in?"

"Fine. Not tonight though. Howie needs to think I'm truly flipping mad."

I frown. "You aren't?"

"Not for me. His disrespect was irritating, but he hit you. That is never okay. I don't care if your father decided to fire him and cut him off. It never was nor will be your fault."

She is everything. Sera will stand in front of me and protect my name when I'm not in the room. I would never let her take a hit for me literally or figuratively. However, her intention is clear. Finding her may be the only good thing that came out of the last tumultuous eight months of my life. While I was in Mystic for only three months, the preceding time before wasn't pleasant and led up to my taking over for a short period. Despite my father's intention to sell the company, working my brother's job was worth it to meet her. "Thank you."

"Always. What else is going on with work? Did you hear about your second offer?"

I drop my head and shake it. I share the details about the deal and who swooped into my spot.

"Have you ever failed to sign a client twice in a row?" Her astute question is the reason I asked my father for the ability to research.

"No. It's suspect in my opinion."

"Will you share your vetting process with me? Maybe for this area you're missing something."

For the next twenty minutes, we talk shop. Her brain is sexy. Sera's insight into the locals is helpful as well. She suggests that fancy dinners aren't the way to go with long established mom-and-pop businesses in the area. She uses our coffee date as an analogy.

"You need to court them a bit differently. Let them see you like I do."

Intrigued, I ask, "How?" That is how I approached the potential clients in the Mystic Cove area.

"You're patient, and it truly is about the client making more money. Sure, you'll benefit, but they will too. You are like Lex. Humble despite having more money than you could possibly spend. Your potential business partners need to see a smart businessman, not hot-as-hell Ashton Calloway in a custom suit they would never be able to afford."

I laugh at the last part. "You kind of like me?"

Sera replies with a laugh of her own. The sound hits me in the chest like it did the first time. "A lot more than kind of."

"Glad we agree. Tell me about your day." I'm falling for Sera. She's kind, smart, and certainly doesn't want my money. Her wealth is more extensive than mine, but she doesn't flaunt it. We're similar in that way. She's a goddess in human form. Most importantly, she cares about me. Sharing my feelings when we're apart for a while seems disingenuous and unfair. The longing is enough as it is, and it's only been a day.

"I went in early to cull the documents in the office and wrap my head around the bookkeeping side of things. Hiring someone is high on my list of priorities, for the store and possibly accounting too. I can't run the store with the back-office duties as well. I could, but it's a lot to juggle. I would need to add focused office time outside of store hours to pull it off. After the holiday, the hours reduce a bit based on past years anyway, but that won't be enough."

"Makes sense. Did Anne have systems in place for new releases and the like?"

"She did. Each month she checked the trades and selected new releases from rising stars or best-selling authors. If Anne missed a hit or one unexpectedly took off, she expedited an order." Her voice drops when she mentions her old boss's name.

"You miss her." The statement leaves no room for explanation, only a single word response.

"Yes."

"Want to talk about her more?"

Sera shakes her head and flops down on her bed. The sight of her in my Columbia hoodie makes me smile. A woman in oversized clothing that belongs to her man hits deep in the heart. If you have the inclination to take it back, she isn't the one.

"When did you steal that?"

My gorgeous woman feigns anger. "Steal? Harsh. I permanently borrowed it.

"Looks better on you anyway. Isn't there some rule about mixing Ivy colors?"

Sera purses her lips, as if she isn't allowed to wear the name of a college other than her alma mater. I burst into laughter. Relief passes over her face.

"I'll willingly give you anything of mine that you want, sweetheart."

She grins. "Same. Although I'm confident nothing in my closet would fit you."

"I don't only mean my clothes," I state to reinforce the blanket permission to use everything I own.

"I know. I should turn in. Please pet Penny for me."

"I will. Only four alone sleeps to go."

Sera blows me a kiss and ends the call. I sigh heavily and trudge out with my dog for a short walk. In this moment, I long for the yard I had at the cottage. I could let Penny run and never leave the warmth of the house. Possibilities about my professional future zip around in my mind. Before I make any decisions about work, I need to determine if Sera is correct about my approach.

CHAPTER SEVENTEEN

SERAPHINA

A mixture of emotions has marked the last few days. I miss Ashton. His smile and support means everything. Unless we were working, we spent every moment together. Sharing my life and space with him made me happier than I have ever been before. Now that he has gone home, time passes slowly despite wishing for the exact opposite.

The good news is he'll be here tomorrow night for dinner. Then we're going to pick up our soirée outfits. We'll likely stay over at Lex's proposal home in Maine. My brother and Keeley knew each other as kids. However, both fell in love with York Beach, Maine. Their time in the area didn't overlap. Once Lex learned of her equal love of the quaint beachside town, he bought her a gorgeous home for them to escape to at will. It's also the site of his second proposal when they realized a marriage of convenience was pointless because they were head over heels in love.

I expect the store to be busy today. Christmas is only two weeks away. The only good thing about Ashton leaving is I can shop freely for him. I'm struggling to find the perfect gift. I purchased two new release thrillers for him already. He isn't the sweater type of guy. I did notice his watch could use replacement. Then an idea dawns on me. I'll do some research and put it into motion as soon as I finish up at Seaside today.

The influx of customers is as expected. I'm running around for the entire day. I'm able to ravenously eat a sandwich Keeley delivered near two.

After completing the purchase for the customer in line, the bell chimes over the door.

I walk toward the customer to offer assistance. Before I get there, a little girl with gorgeous red ringlets is searching frantically in the kid's reading area. I would guess she's about eight years old.

"Can I help you?" I crouch in front of her and her mother.

"I'm Eloise. Where's the fluffy puppy?" Her pout is epic.

Oh my heart. "Penny isn't here today. She had to go visit some family."

"Do you know when she'll be back?"

"No, I don't."

The cute, precocious girl is on the verge of tears.

I quickly add, "What is your mom or dad's phone number?"

Without hesitation, she rattles off two strings of ten digits. The woman beside her, presumably her mother, nods at their correctness.

"I'll text them the next time Penny is here."

She throws her arms around my waist and hugs me. "Thank you. Thank you."

"Of course." I ring up their purchases, and they skip out the door. The remainder of the afternoon passes quickly. Before I walk to my car, I text Ashton.

Me: Can I persuade you to bring Penny to Seaside this weekend?

Ashton: All you need to do is ask.

Me: Eloise was looking for her.

Ashton: Curly red hair?

Me: Yup. I'll call you when I get home.

I have been spending most of my evenings exploring Anne's house. I plan to move there officially after the holidays. I could hire someone for my stuff as well as stock my fridge and pantry. I want to do it myself. The catch is I don't want to give up the time I have with Ashton either.

I stop by the loft and grab clothes for tomorrow. With Thai takeout, I snuggle into the deep chair on the patio at the house. I still can't wrap my head around the fact this belongs to me. Not true. Anne left me her entire estate. Frankly, I didn't think she liked me or cared that much. I was wrong. Reconciling that with our relationship dynamics will take time. Her connection to my grandmother threw me. I nearly reached out to my grandfather but decided not to. There's no doubt in my mind Sumner knew about their friendship, but he never shared. Prior to my father's death, I would consider if my grandfather was playing an angle, whether protecting the family secrets or Celt Industries. More likely, he was shielding his image of his lost love in his heart with no nefarious intent. Also likely is Anne asked him to keep the secret.

My phone chimes beside me.

Keeley: You at the house?

Me: Yeah.

Keeley: I'm on my way.

By the time I wrap up my leftovers and reach the front door, my sister-in-law is climbing the flagstone porch.

"Hi. Everything okay?"

Keeley smiles. Her pregnancy is more evident now. My niece is set to arrive in late summer. "Mostly."

We walked to the kitchen. It's huge with white, floor-to-ceiling cabinetry and Carrera countertops. The pendant fixtures over the island aren't my favorite. However, it is the only issue I have with the kitchen.

"Drink?"

"No, I'm set." She takes a seat at the island. "When are you moving in officially?"

"Probably after the holidays because I would prefer to handle it myself."

She smirks. "You sound like your brother. Billionaires who like privacy and doing the work on their own."

I shrug. Technically, I'm not a billionaire yet.

"It would be easier and faster to hire someone."

"True. Spending money on tasks I can handle seems frivolous to me. What's up?"

"The issue with the container ship is still ongoing. Lex is working with the insurance company. Apparently, Celt has kidnap/ransom and extortion insurance. The agent is negotiating with the pirates for the safe return of the captain's family, the container ship, and the crew. Either way, we're having Kelly send our order for the soirée instead of picking them up. Do you want me to add yours as well?"

While I would like to show Ashton around York Beach, staying here on the first weekend is more appealing. "Yes, that would be helpful."

"No problem. How are you doing?"

I purse my lips and drop my head. "It's crazy to say, but I miss him."

Keeley grins. "Not at all and certainly not to me. When Lex appeared at the café, I was floored. Once I agreed to dinner, I didn't want to spend a moment apart."

"I can't leave Mystic Cove, especially now. He lives in New York. Perhaps before Anne died, I would've considered it. Now, I own my dream and need to continue running it."

"You knew that from the beginning though."

"Fact, but we also believed we had at least three more months to figure out a plan. Now, we're winging it."

"You and Ashton are great together. Plus, your money isn't an issue for him. He has his own. If you want your relationship to work, you'll figure it out."

"Thank you. I like being close to you guys."

She nods furiously. "Me too. Think we could buy the entire neighborhood and convince the others to join?"

I laugh heartily. "Elle isn't far, and she loves her house. Sky definitely won't move. Wave is a wild card. Plus, the upheaval with the trust makes the idea of a family street sticky. Their inheritance is still undetermined."

She frowns. "I forgot about that. Stupid pregnancy brain. I'm more interested in keeping everyone close, not the logistics."

"I love you for it."

While we knew Keeley during childhood, my mother kept her away from us as much as possible. Cecile Soren always reminded us that Cara and her family were "the help." It's unfortunate that Keeley's sister, Fionola, has been uncommunicative for the last ten years or so. Keeley has been caring for her younger brother, Cian, alone. Her older brother, Aidan, was serving in the military overseas until his recent retirement.

"I should get back," she states and pushes off the stool.

We hug, and I escort her to the front door. "Text me when you get home."

"Will do. Say hi to Ashton for me."

I nod and close the door behind her. I set the alarm and climb to my bedroom. I had Jake from Blackthorne check the security system after I confirmed the house was mine.

I flop onto the bed and set two epic gifts in motion with a moderate bit of research. Then I dial Ashton.

He answers nearly immediately. "Hi, beautiful."

The endearment hits me square in the chest. My ex never used them. "How was your day?"

"Decent. You?"

"Busy, but otherwise good. I set up the job posting and found a few purchase offers for Seaside over the years. The most recent was a few months ago. I recall the day because Anne was yelling at the caller, and I overheard her."

"She was adamant about giving Seaside to you."

"She was. What about you? Did you make any progress with your father?"

"Sort of. The time I requested to figure out why my proposals were rejected was granted. The same company approached both the jewelry store and the boutique. My research has stalled because now I need to complete due diligence for the potential sale. I hate it, but I don't have a choice. My father has the final say."

"Is it safe to assume you asked to take over?"

"I did. He refuses to continue if Howie and I aren't on the same page and working well together."

"That hardly seems fair."

"Mitchell Calloway isn't interested in fair. He wants results and to maintain his legacy. Selling before any more bad press or details of Howie's incompetence leaks saves face."

"That sucks for you. I'm sorry." I don't have a direct correlation with Celt, but I can imagine the betrayal Ashton feels.

"Yeah, it does. I follow the rules, stick to the straight and narrow, and it doesn't get me anywhere."

"If you could be anything or do anything, what would you choose?"

Ashton exhales slowly and heavily. "Honestly, I never thought about it. Running the family business was my plan. It may not be an option anymore."

"I understand more than you know. I'm grateful there wasn't a position available for me at Celt when I graduated. More so when my father didn't create one for me. Why don't you buy the company and be your own boss?"

"Intriguing option, which I assure you I'll think more about. I need to get some sleep. I hope to be on my way to you by lunch."

"Love that plan!"

"Me too."

I hear the happiness in his voice at the prospect of seeing me tomorrow. I feel it myself as well. "Can't wait to kiss you."

"Sweet dreams, Sera."

With warm fuzzy thoughts, I plug in my phone and turn in for the night.

Near four, while I'm resetting the nonfiction section in the rear of the store, the door chimes. I remind myself it's too early for him to be here. Then Penny finds me as if she's a trained search and rescue K-9.

I laugh and pet her. Then Ashton appears as if he's on a movie set. He's backlit and looks hot in casual clothes despite the lengthy drive. Ashton appears like the hero at the end of a romcom coming to claim his girl. I'll gladly fill that role as long as he'll have me. *Whoa!*

I rush to him and leap into his arms. Without a doubt, he will catch me. Then I kiss him like it's been years not a week. Relief washes over me before the sheer bliss of his arms holding me close, and our mouths meld together. My emotions aren't in my head at all. We're on the same page at least as far as our relationship. I feel it in his kiss. I watch the clock tick the remaining hours of my workday.

As quickly as possible, we close up the store and race to my loft. It's closer than the house. Once the door snicks behind us, he lowers his mouth to mine and worships it. Containing the whimper when he wet my lips with his tongue is impossible.

Ashton lifts my tee overhead and feasts his eyes on my breasts wrapped in navy French lace.

"Damn! I'll never get tired of finding new lingerie beneath your clothes."

"Don't say things you don't mean!"

"It's worth every penny. Your sexy-as-sin shoes too!"

My cheeks heat up as he dips his head, sucking the curves of my breasts. Hooking his finger under the strap, Ashton pulls it down my arm, followed by his tongue. My nails dig into his back as he bites my nipple hard.

He swirls his tongue around my taut pink bud. I unclasp my bra, dropping it to the hardwood floor. I slip my fingers beneath the hem of his shirt and drag it overhead. I place featherlight kisses across his chest.

"Sera."

He curls his arm under my ass and strides toward the couch. When Ashton sets me on the floor, I slide my hands down the front of his pants and cup his shaft.

"Sera, wait. We're going slow tonight. I missed you. I missed this, and I want to savor it. It may kill me, but I want to explore every inch of you."

I relent because being the center of attention in the bedroom only happens with him. Ashton pops the button of my jeans and pushes them to the floor. I step out of them and kick the denim to the side.

His gaze roams from my brightly red polished toenails, up my long legs, to the matching navy silk thong soaked with need.

"You're staring again."

"No, I'm appreciating you with my eyes, mouth, and hands." He cups my face and kisses me softly before leading me to the bed.

After stepping into the bedroom, I open the snap of his jeans.

"Sera…."

I purse my lips and shake my head. "It's patently unfair that I'll be completely naked in less than a minute and you have half your clothes on. The pants need to go."

"I love you bossy." He throws his hands up in surrender, and I peel his pants down his legs. When I skim my hands up his muscular thighs, his length jumps. "Better?"

"For now."

He tugs me close and wraps one arm around my rib cage. After setting me on the mattress, he climbs up and straddles my thighs. Lifting me once more, Ashton sets me in the center of my bed wearing only my thong.

"Are you trying to kill me?"

Looking up, he replies, "No, I'm taking my time."

Content with his answer, I lay back on the bed. Ashton tucks his fingers beneath the sides of my panties and lowers them toward my feet, kissing and nipping down my leg.

He parts my thighs slowly, making room for his shoulders. Ashton drags his index fingers just outside my core on the left and then on the right. I can't help but squirm. He holds my thigh against the duvet before drawing his tongue from the bottom of my core to the top, sucking my clit between his teeth.

"Ashton."

His name sounds like a plea as he teases me more before dipping his tongue into my folds. It doesn't take long before my legs are trembling and I'm pulling at his hair. Before I recover from those blissful sensations, he pushes two fingers deep into my heated center. I shift forward and back against his hand until I convulse with pleasure.

"Holy hell."

He hums against me, and I writhe against his mouth. After I relax a bit, he climbs up my body, leaving a trail of kisses along the way.

He shimmies out of his boxer briefs as I murmur, "I need—"

Ashton wastes no time. He sheathes his length and pushes into me. I lift my leg onto his shoulder, drawing him further in while curling my other leg around his waist. My inner muscles tighten around him as he thrusts in and out. Shifting my leg from his shoulder, he lifts my hips higher, touching even deeper within me. Waves of pleasure roll through me. Ashton tenses and follows me over the cliff.

Each time I'm with Ashton is more intense and fulfilling than the one before. He slides to the floor and disposes of the condom. He returns with a cloth and cleans me up a bit before wrapping his arm around my waist. Languidly, I roll so I'm on top of him.

Hours later, I wake up with Penny burrowing between us on my bed. I want to yell at her, but her furry face is just so cute. I pretend I don't notice and let sleep overtake me.

Ashton and Penny are spending the day with me at the store. Then we're going to lock ourselves in the house and relax. That was the plan. Instead, we try different positions in most of the rooms, stopping only for food and letting Penny run in the backyard.

CHAPTER EIGHTEEN

ASHTON

After a glorious weekend with Sera spent mostly at the house and claiming every corner from the library to the master balcony, I'm on the road for work. The traveling has fallen on me for our relationship. I don't mind. I'm used to it for my job. It does mean I'm low on sleep today.

This trip I'm in Maryland, then Georgia to check on a few businesses in our portfolio that were under Howie's side of the company. I hope to be back in Sera's arms on Thursday night. I can work from the store on Friday and half the day on Saturday if necessary.

Sounds great, right? The week doesn't go as planned.

"Flight 3234 to BWI has been canceled." A sweet voice over the loudspeaker informs us at the gate. The six-in-the-morning flight that caters to businesspeople is rarely delayed, let alone canceled.

I hurriedly make my way to the counter and request a new flight. Unfortunately, the next one isn't until early evening and will impact my scheduled meeting. I pivot, rent a car, and drive to Maryland instead.

Once I'm on the interstate, I call Sera. "Hi, sweetheart."

"You don't sound happy."

Of course, Sera can hear my displeasure. "I'm not. My flight was canceled. Now I need to hope traffic doesn't make me late."

"That stinks."

"It does, but I get to talk to you again this morning. I'm not mad about it. How are my girls?" I left Penny with Sera rather than board her like normal. Occasionally, my niece can watch her, but she's with Howie for the holiday break. Asking him for a favor right now isn't a great option even if Nina loves Penny. Hell, I'm still waiting for an apology. I'm confident I won't receive it.

I can hear the smile in her voice. "We're great. Penny is on her best behavior. I posted about her presence for the week on the Seaside website. I'll see if she draws more young customers. If she does, as I expect she will, adding story time with puppies or something like that will be in the works."

"Are you stealing my dog?"

Sera sighs. "No, I want to keep you both. I'll probably get one for myself. However, I'm hoping we can figure out a plan to bridge the distance between our homes."

Glad we agree. I hate being away from here especially since it isn't by choice. "Me too. We should discuss it more and soon."

"Drive safely. Good luck with your client."

"Thanks. Talk to you tonight." For the first time ever without travel hiccups, I have limited traffic and am able to make it to the location early. This business is a luxury florist.

I enter the store, which smells glorious and has stations set up for most major events or reasons to give flowers from a funeral to a wedding and every day in between. "Good morning. I have a meeting with Celeste Smith-Hanover." It's barely still morning, but I am on time.

The youngish salesmen dressed in slacks and a polo replies, "I'll get her for you. Your name?"

"Drew Calloway." I use my middle name for business purposes. Actually, for most purposes until I met Sera.

The owner is not what I expected. I anticipated a well-dressed businesswoman. Instead, Celeste's clothing is more casual than her employees with sweatpants and a holey crewneck. "Morning. You aren't Howard."

"My brother was unable to attend this meeting."

She frowns. "I'm confused. You stated you were from Calloway Investments."

"Yes." My gut turns. This can't be good.

"I no longer have a relationship with Calloway Investments."

Fire rushes through my veins. I manage to ask, "Please explain more. Our portfolio indicates your contract doesn't expire for another two years."

"It did until Howard renegotiated a new agreement with me about eight months ago."

He's been stealing from the company while on our payroll. *Murdering my brother would be frowned upon. Right?* Howie left the appointments in the calendar to protect himself. He clearly forgot to remove at least two when my father fired him. "I see. Would you be willing to share the name of your new partner?" I close my eyes and hope she doesn't say HCNC.

My heart drops to my feet when her answer is as I feared.

"NCalloway Corporation."

"Thank you. I appreciate your time and transparency. I'll update our records as necessary."

"Thank you. Have a nice day." She then disappears down the hallway she came from.

I hurriedly exit the shop and call my father.

"Hey, Ashton. How is it going?"

I share the situation with him and add, "I'm going to find out how long Howie has been stealing from our company. Then you are going to threaten to sue him for a litany of things, expose him, terminate his employment, and cut him out of the trust. He clearly believes he can support himself. You can provide for Nina, that's fine, but Howie gets nothing. Then, I'm going to run it myself as I see fit." My tone and words exhibit my anger and borderline hatred for my brother and his actions.

"If you can get evidence, I will do as you ask. Ashton, be sure. This is a one-way street. If you're wrong, Calloway Investments will be sold."

"Deal. Can you give me full access to the financials for the last five years?"

"Consider it done."

"I trust this is between us for now?"

"Yes. This is on you until you have sufficient proof."

"Thank you." With two additional hours on my hands, I return my rental car and set up in the Club at BWI. The lounge provides areas for productivity, relaxation, and food. I'm mostly interested in Wi-Fi to figure out how much my brother has stolen from the company and the timeframe for the same.

First, I investigate the origin of Celeste's new partner. It appears NCalloway Corporation was formed four years ago along with two subsidiaries, HCNC Investments and NinCal Holdings. The timing isn't lost on me. It's right before Christine filed for divorce. I scrub my hand down my face and dig deeper.

Before I get angrier, I call Jake at Blackthorne.

"Hello, Ashton. I'm surprised to hear from you again," Jake answers his cellphone.

"This is for another matter. Sera and I are doing well." I'm falling for her a little more each day.

"Glad to hear it. How can I help?"

"I need a deep dive on my older brother. It appears he has been stealing from the company for an estimated five years. Please bill me personally."

"No problem. Just for your information, Norah generally handles forensic accounting matters. Okay with you?" Norah is his wife of eight years, maybe more. They have three kids. She was a big-shot accountant before a mafia family put a bounty on her head. Since then, she has resigned from her firm and opened a unique bookstore about an hour from here. Her store is a combination of Seaside and Barney's Book Shack with the borrowing option.

"That's fine. Once I have the details, I'll forward it to you," I reply.

"Perfect. I'll update you as soon as I have something."

"Much appreciated, Jake."

I can look at the financial statements and figure out the truth. Norah will be able to do it faster and more precisely, and there will be no wiggle room for my father to save Howie. No space to say I manipulated the data to achieve my personal goals. Do I want to run Calloway? Yes. It was always the plan. Not having my brother as mediocre help may make that impossible. The anger building toward my brother and his choices is simmering below the surface. Rather than show up for a meeting that doesn't exist, I log into my office computer remotely and pull up the internal contact card for the boutique.

"Good afternoon. How may I serve you today?"

Weird for a boutique to answer a call that way, but whatever. "Good afternoon, I'm calling to confirm an appointment with Calloway Investments for tomorrow at 10 a.m."

"One moment, please. I'll connect you."

The hold music is exceptional jazz, which disappears all too soon. "This is Jeanne. We don't have an appointment on the books with Calloway. We signed with their subsidiary NinCal last year." That's how Howie's pulling it off. He's lying to the owners, saying Calloway is restructuring, when in reality he's signing them himself.

"Thank you. Our system has been acting strange, I'll update now. Have a lovely afternoon."

Rather than share the threads I've found with my father, I pack up and change my destination. I'll land in Providence a little after five today and can be at Sera's before seven. Half of me is fuming at my brother, but the rest is excited to sleep beside Sera tonight.

Nearly four hours and a bumpy flight later, my ride greets me at the gate.

"Good evening, Mr. Calloway. May I take your bag, sir?"

"Evening. No, thanks. I can handle it." Hiring a car service is enough rich-guy behavior in one day for me.

Once we're on our way, I text Sera.

Me: Are you at the loft?

Sera: I'm at the house, why?

Me: Want company?

I hope she says yes. Otherwise, I'll need to find a hotel room. She is my girlfriend. We're adults. I'm spiraling for no reason. Something else I can blame on Howie.

Sera: Yes. Is everything okay?

Me: Not sure yet. I'll explain when I get there.

Sera: We're waiting.

The driver pulls up to the front door.

"Have a good evening, Mr. Calloway."

"Thank you. You as well." I open the app and tip him handsomely. Steven was excellent at reading my mood. There was no forced small talk or chitchat. I appreciated it immensely especially after the day I've had.

I knock lightly, and Sera answers the door with Penny at her side. She's a vision in pale pink lounge pants and a matching crewneck.

"Hi."

She opens the door more fully, and I step inside. Penny walks between us toward the kitchen.

"Hi, yourself. Please don't take this the wrong way, but you look like today was hellish."

I frown. "It was. The short version is my brother is stealing from Calloway."

Sera stops in her tracks. "Need a drink?"

"If you have one."

Sera smiles widely, kisses me, and disappears around the corner. A few moments later, she returns with a bottle of Johnnie Walker Blue Label.

"Did you bring that here?"

She laughs, and the sound soothes my aching soul a bit. "No, it appears Anne was a connoisseur of premium wine and liquor. The cellar is stocked with pricey brands and vintages, including some from Braxton Vineyards."

"Nice."

She pours two glasses, and I spill the revelations from the last twenty-four hours. Sera doesn't judge or cast blame on me. She points out the holes in our systems, which allowed Howie to commit fraud and a host of other crimes against his own family.

"What is your plan?" she asks.

I swallow the last sip of the smooth whisky and savor the burn in my chest. "I'm going to get the evidence and stop the sale of Calloway Investments. Norah from Blackthorne is going to do a forensic accounting of the books. I need to send her the data tonight or early tomorrow. Howie will be out of a job and no longer receiving money from the company he embezzled from. Then I will hire a capable second or sell off Howie's side of the portfolio and manage it myself."

Her demeanor shifts slightly.

"What?"

Sera shakes her head. "I completely understand your position, and Howie should no longer work for your family business, nor profit from it, but Nina…."

The fact my niece, a girl she's never met, is her first thought is heartening. "I'll make sure Nina is properly cared for despite her father's stupidity." Her feelings make complete sense. Lex and Sera are supporting their youngest sister and working to find a way to balance the inheritance as best they can. This is a similar situation.

"Good. I'm happy for you. When Mitchell indicated he intended to sell you were pissed. Rightfully so. Now, you don't have to make big changes in your life."

"I do though."

Sera frowns. "Like?"

"When this all works out and I'm in charge, would you be willing to share a room with me in this stunning home?"

She laughs. "Just a room?"

I twist on the stool and turn her to face me. "No. I want you from your polished toes to the tip of your nose and your whole heart. You stole mine after a chance meeting in a park, and I don't want it back."

"Sounds like you love me too."

Sheer joy tumbles in my chest. I lean closer to her and whispers, "I do love you too. I know we're short on hours together, but my heart wants you. I refuse to bottle up my feelings until a more reasonable time to share them. You make me happy. You understand both my personal and business world. I want to hold onto you as long as you're willing to walk with me."

"Let's christen an area of the house and then get some sleep," Sera states with a glint of mischief in her eye.

"Have a specific spot in mind?"

Sera leans closer, a chill zips up my spine, and she whispers, "I'm thinking the library needs some attention."

"I'm in."

My beautiful girlfriend, who loves me in equal measure, hurries to the back door and shoos my dog outside. I'm not sure Penny still belongs to me. She has taken to Sera as well as I have.

When my furry friend returns, we spend the rest of the evening checking off a location in her home. The list will decrease as soon as I can fix the issue with my family business and live here permanently.

CHAPTER NINETEEN

SERAPHINA

Cloud nine is an exceptional place to be. Now I understand what Lex meant when he said he knew in his soul that Keeley was the one for him regardless of the obstacles. Ashton is mine.

He stayed at the house to work while I'm at the store with Penny. I've set up weekly events on Wednesday called "Puppy Reading." We have two slots, one at eleven in the morning and one at four. It allows elementary age children to stop by after school.

The good news is my ad for part-time help received numerous responses. I have three interviews set up for today. For now, I need a capable person to lighten my hours. Working solely with customers during the store hours and then focusing on the business side is a lot for one person. Either way, I'm closing early on Saturday for the Celt holiday party. It irks me, but if my plan to lure my mother works, I need to be there with my guard securely in place. Having Ashton beside me will help.

The first interviewee shows up twenty minutes late.

"I'm so sorry. My car wouldn't start, and I had to figure out a way to get here."

Her excuses won't earn her any points with me. I ask her a few pointed questions specifically about her previous positions and why she left. Brooke solidifies my impression when she shares she was fired for poor attendance. Next candidate, please.

I handle a few customers and sit with Penny while Eloise reads to her in the eleven o'clock session. The sweet ginger has been joining us since the program started.

Her voice drops when she reaches the end of the story. Eloise pets Penny and jumps to her feet. "Will she be here next week?"

"She will," I assure her.

"Yay!" Eloise throws her arms around my waist.

Her mother, Liz, adds, "This program has done wonders for her confidence reading aloud. Thank you."

"You're welcome."

After they leave, I greet my next candidate. He looks familiar. It takes me a minute to place him.

"Ian's older brother?" I recall finding the perfect train book for him.

"Yes. Matt. Thank you for this opportunity."

"Of course. Why work here?"

He's tall, and from my earlier meeting with him, he cares about his little brother. "My mother struggles to provide for Ian on her own. I lost my job a few weeks ago."

I checked his references and former employer. He was a retail associate at a convenience store. The basics are the same as at Seaside. The small family business was forced out by a large chain. In one move, three independent stores were shuttered.

"The basics of this job and your old one would be similar. Are you a reader?"

"Yes, but I usually borrow e-books from the library. It saves money."

I smile and laugh softly. "No worries. The library is one of my favorite places as well. What is your favorite genre?"

"Fantasy and historical fiction."

I'm getting a good vibe from Matt. I'm grateful. A few employees will make my life easier. "Love it. I'm a fan of thrillers and historical fiction as well." I ask a few more questions about whether he was alone at his previous employer and during what hours.

His answers are clear and concise.

"When can you start?"

"Tomorrow?" he asks.

I appreciate his eagerness, and support with the store is welcome. "Perfect. Please arrive at ten in the morning."

"Thank you. I'll be here."

"We will work out a schedule then."

He smiles, stands, and shakes my hand before exiting the store. I round the counter and check my messages.

Keeley: Are you aware Sky and Wave aren't attending the party?

Me: I knew about Sky but not Waverly. I don't blame them.

Keeley: Me either. Hair and makeup at our house at 3.

Me: I'll be there.

I take a few bites of my lunch and message Ashton.

Me: Hey. How's it going there?

Ashton: Good. I sent the reports to Norah and finished a diagram of his organization.

Me: Progress. I had some too. I hired an employee. He starts tomorrow.

Ashton: That's great. You need some support. See you for dinner. Love you.

Me: Love you.

Near three on Saturday, I exit the store with Matt. He's a welcome addition and decreases my stress level significantly. While it may seem premature, I gave him the ability to open or close the store. There's a separate key for the office, which only I have access to. Entering that room no longer holds the same discomfort. Anne was the owner, and that was her space. Now Seaside and the office belong to me.

"I'll see you on Monday." Matt works five days a week with rotating weekends off. He's close to full-time hours, but the schedule allows him to work as a bartender on weekends.

Matt replies, "See you then."

I hurry home, and Ashton greets me at the door with a kiss. We stayed at the house. My furniture and other items are in the loft, but each day, my former boss's home is feeling more and more like my own despite not changing the décor.

"You need to hurry. Keeley already called for you," Ashton states.

I shake my head. "I'm not a fan of this type of event. Despite my wealth, hair and makeup aren't something I enjoy."

He purses his lips. "I know. It's one of the reasons I fell in love with you." He hands me bottled water and shoos me out my own front door. I walk across the street, and Lex greets me.

"You're late," he accuses.

"You too?"

My brother smiles and adds, "I like that guy. Keeley is in the master bath with too many people if you ask me."

"Are you ready for this?"

"No choice. Before you leave to finish dressing, I want to go over the plan."

I dropped my head. "Okay." Part of me wants to end this mess with our mother. The rest would prefer to bury my head in the sand. The latter isn't helpful for any of us, including and especially Lex. The fact he needs to have a son doesn't sit well with me. He also can't change it. Lex can make amendments to eliminate the male-only succession. The snag is Cecile Soren herself. That acknowledgement holds the key.

When I reach the master suite, Keeley is entrenched in her styling session.

"I would hug you, but...."

I wave her off and take a seat beside her.

To be honest, I don't remember the hair stylists names, and that is stereotypically a filthy rich person thing to do. Given my displeasure for this type of attention, I'm giving myself grace.

"How are you feeling?" I ask my sister-in-law while my hair is teased and twisted into an elegant chignon. My dress is navy and off-the-shoulder with a chiffon drape. It's fitted over my curves. I love it. Kelly and her design partner, Billie, never fail.

"Tired, but that's completely normal, or so I have been informed by Elle, Sky, and every article I've read."

"Have you told Cara yet?" Keeley's mom was our housekeeper when I was younger. She's in a memory care facility nearby. Her dementia hasn't progressed rapidly, but she won't recover.

A wave of sadness envelops her.

"I'm sorry." I reach out and cover her hand with mine.

"Not your fault. We told her, but she didn't recall the second time I visited and freaked out about my big belly. That isn't helpful, especially since my weight and curves are an issue for me."

"Cara loves you. She was a great mom." Keeley won't be offended with me using the past tense. The Cara we know and love is gone. My sister-in-law recognizes that fact.

"She does. Ready to see Cecile tonight?"

"I'm hoping she doesn't come."

Keeley laughs heartily. "That woman loves drama and a party. Of course she'll show. I'm still floored she didn't make a grand appearance at my wedding."

"Same. Her presence isn't the issue. It's only when words come out of her mouth that it makes me want to commit violence against her." Attempting to stifle her laugh is impossible for Keeley. "Let it out. Please be prepared in case she needs to be put in her place again."

At their engagement party, my mother brought an eligible, rich woman as her plus-one. Keeley put Cecile Soren in her place on the spot. It was spicy. I hope to have the same gumption if I find myself in a similar position tonight or in the future.

"Hopefully, it doesn't come to that again. I am carrying her grandchild."

I sigh. "You're having a girl. My mother doesn't care about girls one bit."

"I suppose that's true, but we haven't shared the gender with anyone other than the sisters. Besides, you can handle her yourself, especially with Ashton standing beside you."

"That's a plus. Perhaps she won't press you tonight." My face heats at the mere mention of his name.

Our beauty crew is ready to work on our makeup, so the talking needs to end. For the next twenty minutes, they apply and beautify, and Keeley and I sit in silence.

"Miss?" My artist offers me a mirror.

"Thank you." I accept it. Wow, I don't look fake at all. "Perfect. You're amazing."

The young woman nods and smiles. "You're welcome."

I hug Keeley and search for Lex. I find him in his home office.

"You look beautiful."

"Thanks. Your wife puts me to shame."

My brother grins widely. "My plan is to request our mother's signature as soon as she arrives with the caveat she can stay for this party, but it'll be the last one."

"I like it. Ideally, the request and execution will be clean and simple. You're confident she received the invitation and will show?"

"Yes, to the first part. It was hand delivered. Absolutely, she thinks we're going to welcome her back into the fold."

"Where did you find her?"

He smirks, "Blackthorne tracked her to the salon in the Hamptons she's used forever."

"Did you promise her money?"

Lex shakes his head. "No. I merely extended the invitation personally, not from the Celt events office where every other board member's would come from."

"Good. I need this to end for us and for our sisters."

His lips pull into a tight line. "This is only step two or three. It gives me the power to move forward on the business side and with the trust."

"I know. It sucks all around that she's holding us hostage, if you will. It's completely her fault the estate and trust are playing out this way."

"Yeah. You should get going. Sumner won't be happy if we arrive after Cecile."

I laugh heartily. "I would love to be a fly on the wall for that conversation."

"Me too."

I hurry home and find Ashton sitting in the library mostly dressed. The only thing missing is his jacket.

"You're hot!"

"Your hair and makeup are on point. I hung your dress in the walk-in closet after steaming it."

"You're the best! I'll be down in fifteen minutes, max."

Ashton chuckles, and I hustle upstairs. When I reach my bedroom, I'm floored. Not only did he steam my dress, but he pulled out the three shoe options we discussed, which will keep me at or below his height, and laid out lingerie options that work with my dress. He's perfect for me. Each time he cares for me or makes my life easier solidifies my love for him.

Tonight will be stressful for both of us. He's going to meet Sumner, but that will be cake compared to the confrontation with my mother. I opt for the black set, change, and step into my dress. I zip up the side, slip on my Kate Strauss sparkly pumps, and return to my man on time.

Ashton rises from the couch and stalks toward me. "Wow! You look fantastic!" He leans forward to kiss me but stops short. "I don't want to wrinkle you, but I want to smear that lipstick."

"Thank you. As do you. Go ahead, ruin the lipstick. I have more."

He needs no further assurance. Ashton hauls me into his arms and kisses me to breathlessness. The rush of endorphins makes me relax instantly, and I'm ready to tackle this event.

We arrive shortly before five and are greeted by Walter.

"Miss Soren. Mr. Calloway. Pleased to see you again."

I look left, then right and hug him. "Hi, Walter. How are you?"

He winks. "Still here and kicking. Pleasure to meet you." He extends his hand to Ashton.

"I've heard great things about you from Sera and Lex."

Walter grins. "None of it is true." Then he tilts his head in jest. "Mr. Soren and Mrs. Lange are in the solarium."

"Thank you. I remember the way. Happy Holidays, Walter."

"To you as well." With our fingers threaded together, I give Ashton a tour of the estate as we walk to the party. It's brief but does the job.

"Just to verify, that's Ellery."

"Yes."

"Does your grandfather live here alone? This home is stunning but massive."

"Sumner and Walter are the only people who remain. There are a few staff who check in during the week, like the cleaning crew and the gardener when seasonally appropriate." I squeezed his hand. "Ready for this?"

"I can do anything with you."

For now, I'm just a female heir and nothing more. Where my grandfather sits on the changes Lex intends to make isn't public knowledge. We greet my sister and then I introduce my boyfriend to Sumner.

"Grandfather, please meet Ashton Calloway."

They shake hands. Sumner is thin, and I make a mental note to talk to Walter and Lex about his health. For a man of his age, he's healthy. Then again, so was Anne.

"Pleasure to meet you, young man."

"You as well, sir." They chat about the market and the press when Howie hit Ashton. "We are dealing with it as discreetly as possible."

"As you should. Hiding the black sheep is difficult under the best circumstances and disastrous under the worst."

My grandfather would know. Soren secrets were his domain. Luckily, we have unearthed the remaining lies and deceit. *I hope there aren't any more.* Now, we need to deal with them one by one. Tonight, the best outcome would be for my mother to move on.

The high-pitched tone echoing down the hall would indicate she has arrived.

Ashton unlinks our fingers and slides his arm around my waist. "We've got this."

"She showed," Sumner grumbles.

I lean closer and whisper, "Ideally, it'll be the last time she ever steps foot in this place."

"From your lips, my dear," Grandfather replies.

Cecile Soren breezes into the solarium. As she does, silence befalls the room. Like when she arrived at Seaside, she's dressed to the nines, including a different luxury handbag.

"Where is Lexington? He demanded my presence but didn't bother to show up." Her voice reverberates like nails down a chalkboard.

"We're here. Had a bit of car trouble," my brother responds as he enters the room.

I glance at Keeley and note that she looks flushed. The car is fine. My sister-in-law isn't. Lex shakes Ashton's hand and hugs me.

Then I hug Keeley and ask quietly, "Are you okay?"

She mouths, "I'm fine now." I surmise she had a bout of morning sickness, which has seemed to stick with her. The name is a myth as it occurs at any time of the day.

"Well, good of you to show up. I would suggest you get a new car, but that wouldn't serve you. Spending the family fortune isn't something you're keen on doing."

"Hello, Mother. Lovely to see you again," Lex replies, but he's clearly bristled by her presence despite the necessity.

"Always is. I was surprised by your invitation. I hope you have reconsidered my request."

What request? I'm not shocked she hasn't acknowledged my presence. It stings even if Lex has always been the favorite child. I stand tall and listen intently.

"No, I have not changed my mind."

"Then why am I here if not to get a piece of the Soren fortune?"

I step forward in a moment of boldness and lunacy. "You're here to do what my father wanted."

"Give up?" she asks. "Never."

Lex offers a little context. "I'm unable to make any more decisions or corporate moves until you execute the acknowledgement. A fact you are well aware of. There is no compensation for doing what you're required to do as delineated in the bylaws. You chose this path. I'm merely enforcing the rules required by my role in this company."

"Can't you see? We won't capitulate to your requests anymore," I add.

For whatever reason, that statement my mother heard clearly. Yet, she doesn't address me. She speaks to Ashton instead. It's as if I'm not even here.

After looking him from head to toe, she says, "You're still around. That's a shock. Seraphina is the most difficult of my daughters to please."

My entire body tenses. "I'm not. I have standards and boundaries, as everyone should."

"Ma'am, my relationship with Sera is none of your business. You have made it clear that your fortune, or lack thereof, and power is more important than mending fences with your children. While I do not speak for Sera, I would prefer not to engage with you again, especially considering the manner in which you treat her."

Cecile scoffs. "How would you know?"

"I was present when you showed up at Seaside. Yet, you were so entrenched in your words you didn't hear me enter the store. The disrespect you exhibited toward your daughter was unfathomable. She's an adult and has no control over you at all. Yet, you seem to thrive on making chaos wherever you appear. None of your children deserve such treatment."

"How dare you speak to me in such a manner."

A sexy twinkle—which shouldn't register at this moment—appears in his eye. "I have nothing to lose by sharing my true feelings about you."

Cecile grits her teeth and replies, "I'll make sure Sera leaves you."

"Like hell you will." Despite my couture gown and meticulously applied makeup, I defend my relationship loudly and with pride. "I choose Ashton. I don't need your approval or permission. Please do what Lex asked and leave. You gain nothing by refusing to sign. There is no money, real estate, or prestige for you here anymore. The only hold you have is making it difficult for Lex to run Celt efficiently and properly. Sign so we can avoid a nasty court battle where all your secrets will come to light."

Her dirty laundry still might become known when my sisters search for their fathers, but I don't divulge that at this moment. Chances are, her baby daddies are wealthy men. They would want to keep their indiscretions hidden in equal measure as my mother. These revelations will make headlines. As much as I would like to think her signature will sever ties with Cecile Soren for good, I'm not hopeful. It will help Lex move forward with Celt though.

My mother inhales sharply and looks between me and my brother. Ellery is off to the right, watching this discussion. Her arms are folded tightly over her chest. I suppose signing her name will admit what we already know. There are two distinct groups of her children. The acknowledgment, though not explicitly, states exactly that.

Lex reaches into his jacket pocket and produces an envelope with the Celt logo in the corner. He takes a step to his right toward the Henry VII era credenza against the wall.

She scoffs and joins my brother. My mother mutters something I can't hear and then extends her hand. With a pen provided by my brother, she scribbles her name at the bottom of the page. The silence in the room is deafening. There will be no applause or compensation for compliance.

She looks at Sumner, who watched stoically as this confrontation went down. "I never liked you."

"Feeling is mutual. You are no longer welcome in my house."

My mother huffs, turns on her red-soled heels, and exits the family mansion for the last time. Sumner Soren doesn't go back on his word. Ever.

Thankfully, this is a family owned and operated company. The only person present at this event without any personal stake—financially speaking—was Ashton.

Silence falls over the room. The clock ticking on the sideboard is the only sound.

Grandfather breaks the tension. "Dinner is served."

Chatter begins, and we file into the dining room.

"How are you?" Ashton asks while we walk.

"With her, I'm the same. She's my mother, but I can't imagine treating my children with such disdain. I'm grateful she signed so Lex can move forward. With you... thank you for standing up for me."

"You did just fine on your own. I refuse to allow anyone to demean or disrespect my partner. It was difficult not to punch Howie to defend your honor."

"I appreciate it more than you know. I love you."

"You did the same for me. I love you."

The mood shifts from shock to cordial revelry once the meal is served and we realize this part of our story is over. Cecile Soren no longer has any foothold in Celt Industries. Lex can make the necessary changes to the bylaws to allow a woman to take over. It likely won't be me, but the fact it will be possible makes me happy. Truth be told, I don't want to run the company, I never did. He can also expand on his philanthropic endeavors without interference.

Tonight feels like a step forward for the Soren family. The sad part is progress for the Sorens means separation as well.

CHAPTER TWENTY

ASHTON

The Soren family certainly knows how to handle their business in private. When Sera suggested subterfuge to get her mother to sign, I was skeptical. Why would a woman need urging to do the right thing for her children? For Cecile Soren, she was differentiating between her offspring on paper. The fact is… she made that decision long ago. The event a few nights ago was simply the culmination of her life choices.

Sera handled herself with grace. Her poise made me fall deeper in love with her. If she can stand up to her mother without name-calling and underhanded deeds, then my woman is an asset personally and professionally.

My family, on the other hand, remains a work in progress. Norah made some preliminary findings that don't bode well for Howie. At a minimum, he created upward of four companies and was actively seeking to shift Calloway clients to himself. Norah requested another week to complete her investigation. She felt a heads-up was necessary to prevent any further damage to Calloway. I appreciate the notice. To that end, I decreased his access to anything pertaining to my side of the business, including research stored on the company server.

I need to determine how my brother is using the company data. I requested complete access to the company system. My father granted it reluctantly. Blaine, Blackthorne's investigator, will be able to track Howie's movements and provide proof. Like Norah's work, an outside third party is necessary to solidify my fears. Howie is stealing clients and using Calloway's goodwill, reputation, and work product to do it. Maintaining my composure without showing up at his ostentatious home is a side effect of being in Mystic Cove. If I wasn't with Sera, I would be at my apartment and close enough to pop by unannounced and hurl accusations at him. Not having a vehicle here now is a blessing in disguise. Driving thirty minutes in New York traffic is one thing. Three hours plus is another. Howie is lucky I fell head over heels for Sera and we can work remotely.

Sera has made progress in fully moving into the house. The main level office, which Anne was using as a bedroom, has been returned to its original purpose. While the furnishings and color palette are decidedly feminine, I have been using the space as an office. My phone chimes while I'm deeply entrenched in check-ins for my clients.

Sera: How is it going?

Me: Good. You?

Sera: Slaying dragons with Penny and Eloise.

Me: Love it.

Sera: The weekly event is a great success because of you.

Me: It's fair to say Penny is ours.

Sera: Awww. See you later. Love you.

Me: Love you.

With a boost of serotonin, I call Lex before diving back into my work.

"Hi, Ashton. Everything okay with Sera?"

"Yes. Sorry. No need for alarm. My breeder reached out. She has six available puppies. Each is trained for basic commands and crate trained."

"Of course." I hear relief in his voice. "I would like two for our house. Ellery and Sky are each in for one."

The remaining two are for Sera. She'll be able to expand her puppy reading event. "I'll arrange for delivery. Does your home address work during the family celebration?"

"Yes, that would be perfect. All my sisters will be here."

"Consider it done."

Lex replies, "Let me know the balance, and I'll take care of it. Also, what time are we meeting for the festival?"

"At Seaside, Friday at six. Are the kids coming too?"

"Yes, everyone will be there, including Aidan and Cian."

Inwardly, I frown. "Who are they?"

"Sorry, Keeley's brothers. Aidan recently retired from the military, and Cian lives at Maple House, which caters to adults with autism. It provides support and job training as well as a sense of community."

"Can't wait to meet them. See you then."

I end the call and immediately reach out to my contact at Sugar Hill Farms and arrange for the entire litter to be delivered this weekend. It's a bit early, but the Sorens are getting together then because Ellery's kids are with their father this year. I completely understand. Nina will be with Howie this year, and we are celebrating on the holiday. I place an order for new puppy supplies and get back to work until Sera arrives home for the day.

I hoped I would get away without speaking to my father again before our visit next week. I want more proof to support my bid to take over the company. His call is unsettling.

"How is your preparation going for the potential buyers?"

"I'm about fifty percent complete."

"Good."

I tamp down the anger swelling in my gut. "Dad, it is a fruitless endeavor. I won't let you sell the family business because you refuse to believe I'm right about Howie."

"There isn't a choice. Assuming you're correct, selling is the only option."

"Why? I'll hire a capable second."

"You can't, at least not with how the bylaws are structured. The bylaws require anyone drawing on the trust to be directly involved in the company. The trust is funded mostly by Calloway Investments."

"There has to be a section dealing with malfeasance."

"There is. I'm not sure it applies to your brother anymore after I demoted him."

Containing my displeasure is no longer an option. "You made it impossible for me to continue Calloway Investments because you didn't do your due diligence?"

"It's possible, yes. I took the easy route, and it may cost us."

"Not us. Me. I have never steered wrong for this family or the company. I did what was expected of me, and now you're saying, it doesn't matter. I'm going to lose everything I earned for because Howie is a thief and liar! You missed it, and I'm going to suffer."

"It's probable. I'm sorry, Ashton."

I scrub my hand down my face. "Please confirm I have access to the trust and bylaws on the company server. I'm going to end this call before I say something I regret. I'll get you the evidence and the prospectus for a buyer. Please figure out a way to change the bylaws or the trust so our family business doesn't crumble to rubble."

I push end and resist hurling my phone across the room by the slimmest of margins. Instead of continuing work, I change and go for a long run despite freezing temperatures. A bit of my anger leaves my body with each strike of my feet on the cold pavement. The cold air in my lungs feels great now but will induce coughing later. After three miles, I turn back toward Sera's. The first step is a thorough reread of the documents controlling my life. Then a new game plan.

I won't start this until after Sera goes to sleep or tomorrow. Despite the turmoil with my business, I won't sacrifice my time with her when she's home. It's a huge deal for me and may impact my decisions going forward. Could I simply start my own company? Live off my trust for a bit and work at Seaside? There are plenty of options. The only thing I know for sure is I want Sera in my life.

SERAPHINA

String lights hang from the trees above, the ground is covered with white paint and fake snow, and classic holiday songs play through the speakers. Row upon row of vendors line the fairgrounds with gift ideas galore, and a few groups of young children sing carols on a stage near the rear of the festival. These talented chefs bring it all. This year the organizers have added s'mores row, or so I've heard. Five bonfires are set up and dutifully guarded by members of the Mystic Cove Fire Department.

"I'm so excited to do this with everyone this year."

"Same here." My sisters agree.

The kids are amidst the group laughing along with Aidan and Cian.

I shop the holiday crafts, handmade blankets, and scarves with Sera. Before we head over to the food section, Sky and I pop into a photo booth and laugh through the shutter snaps.

"He makes you happy, Ser," my sister states.

The booth captures my smile with the next image. "Ashton is… everything I was looking for without family money."

"I get it. You wanted a normal guy. Ashton is Lex but not related to you."

I laugh heartily, and the last image is taken. Sky is absolutely right. "You will find someone again, sis."

Her shoulders drop. "I'm not in a hurry. I still miss Silas every single day. When Lia does something ordinary, I have the urge to tell him. I do but in my thoughts." My sisters are the strongest women I know. Sky tops the list hands down. We hug and then my man exchanges places with her.

"Hi, gorgeous. Miss me?"

I kiss him as the booth snaps a photo. Then I laugh and reply, "Yes."

We pose for the next image with my head on his shoulder.

"We don't have festivals like this near home. It's awesome. The activities and…"

Snap!

I giggle and then we stare at each other for the last photo.

We hop out and wait for the sheet to print. Ashton slips the strip into his pocket.

"Let's go."

We traipse up and down each row until we settle on our dinner option. I choose macaroni and cheese topped with bacon while Ashton selects a pulled pork sandwich with fries. When the guys are sufficiently full—for now—we hop in line for the icicle maze. It's a take on a corn maze for the winter. The walls are covered in glittery-white fabric, and the clues are holiday trivia. Ellery splits up the family members. Given the imbalance of gender, she mixes based on age.

My team includes Ashton, Cora, Cian, Wave, Keeley, and me. Our opponents are Lex, Ellery, Weston, Aidan, Sky, and Lia. Keeley and Ellery are dark horses in any trivia game, so this should be interesting. However, I have a secret weapon on my team; Wave loves Christmas and is the early decorator in the family.

"What are the stakes?" Keeley asks before we enter the maze.

"Losers buy dinner at Braxton Vineyard for the winners," Ashton suggests.

A chorus of "Yes" echoes through the group. We grab our sheets from the worker and take off into the maze.

I read the first question. "How many states grow Christmas trees?" Silence—I'm met with silence. "Come on, Wave. You're the queen of Christmas."

"No idea," Cian offers.

"Same. Guess, Wave," Ashton states.

"All of them?" Wave questions.

"Turn right." We walk in a cluster to the next checkpoint. A group of high schoolers whoosh past us before I can read the clue.

"How many gifts would you receive if you received all the 'Twelve Days of Christmas?'" Keeley asks the group.

"Three hundred sixty-four," Ashton announces.

"How did you do that so fast?" Wave asks.

He shrugs. There's a story there. "Someone double-check my math."

Cian pulls out his phone and adds it up. "Well done. Three hundred sixty-four is the answer." Aidan checks over his brother's shoulder.

"Left turn." We successfully answer three more questions about basic Christmas lore by naming the reindeer as well as Rudolph's father. It's Donner, if you're keeping score. At our sixth station, I'm sure we're going to be stumped. "What is the name of the Grinch's dog?"

Crickets. Nothing but crickets.

I huff. "Come on, guys! This one is easy."

Ashton lowers his lips near my ear. "You flustered with the answer is sexy as hell."

"It's short and begins with an M," Wave mutters. "Wait, wait! It's Max."

"Yeeesssss, sis!" I give her a side hug, and we laugh our way to the next clue. Both groups arrive at the same point at once.

"Ready to go down?" Lex asks.

"Never!" I reply.

"How do we make this fair?" Ellery asks. "We arrived here at the same time."

"We both read the questions and have thirty seconds to come up with the answer. If we don't, we lose. If we tie, we read another question until someone doesn't know. That work?"

"Let's get this done. There are s'mores to be eaten," Weston whines.

Aidan continues, "What popular toy did everyone want in the movie *Jingle All the Way*?"

Ashton does the honors for our team, "What does Santa give as the first gift of Christmas in *The Polar Express*?"

I know both answers! Dinner out, here we come. The groups huddle up and whisper amongst themselves.

"Time's up!" Ellery announces.

"Our answer is a silver sleigh bell. What's yours?" I ask.

The group hangs their heads, and Sky states, "We don't know."

"Woo-hoo!" I cheer.

Ashton pulls me closer and presses a kiss to my temple.

"Wave?" Sky asks.

"Turbo Man action figure," she replies and high-fives me.

We make our way to the bonfire area and peruse the buffet-style table holding the ingredients.

"Are we going with original or peanut butter s'mores this evening?" my gorgeous man murmurs before kissing my cheek.

"Schuyler, is that you?" a voice I can't readily place calls from my right.

My sister turns and smiles. "Beckett." She hugs him and introduces him to my family. I don't miss Aidan bristling with something... jealousy or interest or perhaps both.

"Everyone, this is my neighbor, Beckett."

Beckett Lauder is a local. His son attends school with Lia. His dusty blond hair and striking blue eyes are a potent combination. Aidan appears to relax when his shoulders drop. I believe he's wrongly assuming Beckett is married. Someday a woman is going to be lucky to call Aidan hers. He's tall, dark, and handsome and the complete opposite of Beckett. After my earlier conversation with Sky, neither has a shot, at least not anytime soon.

Beckett tags along as we walk to the café where my family parked. Lia and Beckett's son, Cal, are chatting away.

"Time to say goodbye, Cal," Beckett states.

Cal hugs Lia, and they cross the street toward additional parking. The rest of us say our goodbyes, knowing we'll be spending the day together tomorrow complete with excellent food and gifts for the kids.

CHAPTER TWENTY-ONE

SERAPHINA

Creak! Damn it! I need to get used to the floors and where the pitfalls lie.

"Morning," Ashton mumbles.

"Sorry. I'll be back as soon as possible. I need to take Penny with me." I kiss him lightly.

"Okay," he mutters and returns to sleep.

With coffee from Anne's fancy machine, I leave with Penny in tow. I always wondered why she never went to the café. Anne has the same espresso machine as Keeley. Ashton figured out how to use it. He's working on his menu items when he can. My own personal barista has moved into my house. Sigh.

The twinkle lights outside the store are shining when I arrive. Matt beat me here this morning, and I'm fine with it. He's an asset. Unlike my relationship with Anne, I'm getting to know him.

"Morning," I greet him while Penny rushes inside and clamors for attention.

"Hey!" He squats and ruffles the top of her head.

"How was your brother's chorus concert?"

His unique green eyes soften. He towers over me, and I'm not a short woman. "If I'm being honest, it was terrible. Those cute kids have no clue how to harmonize."

I laugh. "Fair observation."

I learned from his application, he's twenty-two. He's a trained electrician from trade school but can't put in the time for apprentice hours. He works here, picks up his brother, Ian, during the week and cares for him at night. It allows his mom to hold down two jobs. I haven't had the heart to ask about the missing dad. As much as I would hate to lose him as an employee, I hope he's able to get back to his profession sooner rather than later. Maybe when Ian is a bit older.

A fiery head of red hair bursts into the store.

"Hi, Wave. What are you doing here?"

"Is that the best way to greet your sister?" she jokes.

"I expected you to be sleeping in and then getting ready for Lex's later."

She taps her finger on her lower lip while keeping time with her foot on the hardwood floor. "I need a last-minute gift for this afternoon."

I smile. "For?"

"I can't tell you who my recipient is," she reminds me. We each pick an adult and have a spending limit. We get together and buy a gift for the kids. Keeley is on wrapping duty this year. "Got it. Matt, could you assist my younger sister?"

"Sure." When Matt fully looks up at Wave, I see low-key interest. *Cool.*

I take a seat in the office and pull reports as well as clear the messages. Nearly an hour later, Matt and Wave are still chatting near the fiction section, but she already bought some books. They would make a gorgeous couple.

Right before "Read with Penny" begins, Eloise and her father stand in line. A few more kids join. I didn't think this program would take off quite so well. Adding a puppy or two is now a necessity.

Eloise, Jack, Kyle, and Caroline read aloud to Penny. The kids each reciting different books is difficult on their ears, but for now it's what I can pull off. I chat with the parents and assure them I'm keeping the program in the rotation and they should check the website for the schedule. I don't foresee Ashton leaving anytime soon. I love having him in my life.

The other bonus of having Matt at Seaside is he keeps me on schedule. He approaches the group and reminds me I have an appointment.

"Please excuse me. Happy Holidays!" I mention to the group before turning to Matt. "Thank you. My family will be angry if I'm late."

Matt smiles. "Your sister said the same thing. Have a great time. I'll see you next week."

"I appreciate you." I clip on Penny's leash, and we rush out of the store. When I arrive home, Ashton is waiting for me. Odd but I am pushing it a little.

"You made it." He kisses me and offers me his arm.

"Barely. Matt deserves the credit. He reminded me."

Ashton nods. I appreciate that he isn't the jealous type. Matt is good-looking, nice and charming. I'm not interested in him at all. My little sister on some level might be, but I won't meddle.

Loaded down with gifts, we walk to Lex and Keeley's. Wave is going to lose her mind when she sees the decorations. Lights and deer are scattered across the lawn. There's a small barn with woodland creatures. Wave is a Christmas fanatic. When we were little, before boarding school, she would wake each of us up and drag us to the tree. That probably only happened two or three times at most given the age gap between her and Lex. The sheer joy on her face is impossible to ignore.

"Your brother goes all out," Ashton commented.

"It's for Wave, but yeah."

Of the Soren siblings, she's the likeliest to lose the most. As far as the distributions are concerned, the attorneys are working out our options. Ideally, they will come up with a plan that can meet what Lex and I want to do. The legal team has suggested we push off deciding as long as possible. It gives Lex and Keeley time to have a son, and the lawyers gain space to create the best overall outcome. My trust is unaffected by the turmoil with the estate. Lex and I will find a way to make it as fair as possible for our sisters.

The front door swings open, and Cora greets us. More accurately, she wants Penny snuggles.

The smells of a fabulous meal hit me when I step inside. No doubt my brother has been in his gourmet chef's kitchen since dawn. While he's a master in the boardroom, his passion is cooking.

The house is bustling with activity. The only person who hasn't arrived yet is Wave. Even Aidan and Cian are already here.

"Nice to see you again, Cian," Ashton greets him.

"I like him, Aunt Sera. He 'member me too." Keeley's younger brother is autistic and lives in a nearby supportive home. He has made great strides getting a job and contributing to the community.

I lean in as if it were a secret. "I do too."

While we chat, Ashton and Aidan are talking about the football schedule for today. That sport isn't my thing, but apparently Aidan is a die-hard Bears fan like my sister, Sky.

As we make our way farther into the house, Keeley and Sky appear and disappear after short greetings. My sister-in-law running around makes sense but not Sky. I shrug it off and talk with Cora and Cian while they entertain Penny.

"Why is she tired, Auntie?" Cora asks.

I smile. "My readers tuckered her out today. She's going to need a friend or two to handle the lucky kids who want to read stories."

"I asked Mom for a puppy for Christmas. I don't know if it'll happen though. Can I visit yours when you get it?"

"Sure, sweetie. Anytime."

Lex walks through the curved archway and announces, "Dinner is served."

A roar of laughter passes through us, and we follow in a perfect line like soldiers into the elegantly decorated dining room. Keeley created place cards for the occasion. The placement is intriguing as well. Lex and Keeley are side by side, and the family fans out from there. Cian is next to her, then Aidan. Sky is beside him. My sister-in-law may be playing matchmaker on the sly. I don't hate it. They make a gorgeous couple. Plus, Aidan's attentiveness to Cian is a great indicator of his inclination toward parenthood.

The sounds of silverware on plates and a few laughs here and there mark an excellent meal. Truly, we're here for the gifts. The kids are at least. The three of them have eaten, cleared their plates, and joined the adults again to wait patiently.

For Lia that means swinging her feet to and fro beneath the table.

"I'm done," Cian states. He rises and brings his dish into the kitchen. "Keeley, can we use the sunroom?"

Before she can answer, Aidan pipes up. "I'll go with them as long as it's okay with you." The latter part of his question is directed at Sky.

"Thank you for checking. Sure, Lia."

My niece hops off her chair and takes Cian's hand.

Aidan grabs his plate, but Sky covers his hand with hers. "I'll take it."

He nods tightly and follows the kids out of the dining room. The blush on my sister's face is fierce. I don't address it in the moment. When the remaining adults finish eating, the ladies wash the dishes except Keeley. We laugh and joke. When we're nearly done, I notice both Lex and Ashton are nowhere to be found.

"Where did the guys go?" I ask.

I'm answered by a chorus of "I don't know." My curiosity is piqued, but I don't search for them. Instead, I scope out the table full of Keeley's treats.

There are staples, including chocolate mousse pie and pumpkin pie, but the fruit tart and filled croissants look new.

Lex and Ashton return shortly thereafter and announce it's gift time. In the rush of hoots and hollers, mostly from the kids, I go with the flow.

The group shuffles into the main living room. Like the outside, it looks as if a holiday movie set threw up in here. I can see my sister chilling in this space each morning with her coffee. Wave would be comfortable in a year-round Christmas-themed film. She's staying with our brother for semester break. He has plenty of space. She did ask to live at the loft after graduation. I'm excited to have her close to home again.

Weston sits on the edge of the chair. Patience is not his strong suit.

Lia pipes up first, "What are the numbers?"

The adults laugh, and Ellery answers, "We already picked them. Now we share the gifts."

"Yay!" She claps her hands and sits beside Penny on the floor. Interestingly, Aidan is the nearest adult as far as proximity. Her comfort level with him isn't surprising though. While she was young, she knew her father was in the military. Aidan exudes structure and discipline. It doesn't hurt he's hot as hell… for my sister of course.

Ashton's fingertips gliding along my arm capture my attention. He is engrained in my life now. I notice when he isn't touching me.

"Where did you and Lex run off to?"

My man with a blue sweater that makes his eyes pop shrugs and adds nothing more.

The adult exchange is generally fast and light-hearted. Keeley found the perfect briefcase for Wave and had it personalized with her monogram. That is bittersweet. My younger sister seems to love it though. Ellery opens the historical fiction books Wave purchased earlier today. My gift was a spa manicure and pedicure. I will likely never use it, but I enjoy the idea of being pampered.

The room stands still when Aidan, whose shock would indicate he didn't expect a gift, receives a shadow box with his military medals displayed.

Lia hops to her feet and leans closer to Aidan. "We have one of those for my daddy."

Sky immediately crosses the room and whispers a few words to Aidan.

I couldn't hear them, but I could read his response. Along with his surprise, he's touched. "No problem. She's fine."

My sister sits back down in her seat, and we continue the gift exchange. While the family's attention was on Ellery opening her gift, my focus oscillates from Aidan and Lia to Sky. He sits on the floor beside her and shares information about each medal.

When Sky sees their interaction, her shoulders sink, and her eyes tear up before she leaves the room. I stand to go after Sky, but Aidan says something to Lia. She hugs him, and he follows my sister's exit. My sister is firmly against dating another military man, but my niece is drawn to Aidan.

Luckily when the remaining exchanges are complete, Aidan and Sky return. My sister's face is mildly puffy, but she's not crying anymore. Whatever Aidan said soothed her at least for now.

I mouth, "You okay?"

Sky acknowledges me with the tilt of her head. She's not okay overall, but she is for now at least.

Lex and Ashton rise to their feet.

My brother says, "If everyone could follow us, there is one more gift to give."

Giddy with anticipation, we follow the guys to the garage. As we walk, I thread my fingers with Ashton's.

"What is going on?"

"You'll see."

Six sweet pups with big bows are playing in a small playpen area. Joy zips through me, and I'm not even sure one of the fluffy puppies is for me.

"Who gets a new friend?" Cora asks.

Ashton answers, "You and Weston and Lia get to choose. Then the rest are for Sera and Keeley."

I lean in near his ear and say, "You got me a puppy?"

He winks. "Two actually."

I pepper his cheek with kisses while the kids are playing with the pups. "Are they siblings?"

"Yeah. There are two boys and four girls," he answers.

I don't mind waiting for the kids to choose first. Although secretly, I'm eyeing the tiniest runt in the group.

"You should join them," Ashton urges.

I grab Keeley's hand, and we step over the small wall and sit with the kids.

Giggles and smiles are high right now. The runt has cozied up to my leg, and two others have wandered in our direction.

"What about this one, Cor?" Weston snuggles one of the male dogs. I love that he is working with her to decide.

Cora shifts next to him, and the pup climbs into her lap and begins licking her face. She laughs. "Sure."

With that decision made, Lex clips a blue collar and leash around their gift. I hear them bantering about a name.

Sky and Lia choose as well. A female pup they quickly name Sadie. Lex gives her the red collar.

That leaves Keeley and I to select our new fluffy friends. "Have a front runner?" I ask my sister-in-law.

"Not really. Why don't we trade off? You go first."

I smile at her and select the female runt. Ashton adds a purple collar and snuggles her a bit. I'm going to have to work on what to call her and her companion I have yet to select.

Sooner than I thought, it's my turn again. I opt for the regal-looking male watching over the group. Ashton gives him a blue collar.

"I can't believe you pulled this off with my brother," I state with our female in my arms and him holding the male.

"To be honest, I started the whole thing. I called my breeder after Penny's first visit to Seaside."

"Really?" I kiss his cheek.

"Yeah. Lex added to the request at Thanksgiving for Keeley. Sky and Ellery weren't hard to convince either."

"Is this why you were acting odd earlier and where you disappeared to with my brother?"

"Yes and yes. The puppies were in your garage. We moved them here when we snuck out a little while ago."

"Well played."

Ashton grins. "Thanks."

"Do you still want to wait until next week for your gifts?" I ask.

"Yes. I have a few more for you too."

I shake my head in disbelief. "I think these two are plenty." Our female squirms in my arms. I set her down and drop the leash so she can roam around.

Ashton slides his arm around me and kisses near the top of my cheek. "That is one of the reasons I love you. You don't need anything from me, which makes me want to give you everything."

"Same for me."

I'm surprised, but Lex and Keeley allow all the new puppies into the house while we have dessert and spend the rest of the evening together. Like other holidays, we devour the delicious foods and play cards. Only today, there are six furry companions adding to the fun.

CHAPTER TWENTY-TWO

ASHTON

The last few days have passed in a blur regarding information on my brother and his malfeasance and integrating two new pups to our morning routine. Norah provided her report. I'm sick to my stomach reading the details. How on earth did my father miss all this? Monitoring Howie was never my responsibility until recently. I don't want to cast blame solely on him, but the truth is that's where it falls. Unfortunately, my father misplaced trust in my brother. It makes me angry and sad at once.

My hands shake as I review the innerworkings of the corporate structure my brother created to steal from the family business. He started this six years ago, before his divorce. My former sister-in-law has no idea she was fleeced along with the Calloway Investments. I'm confident of that fact. Christine is a nice person and a good mother. Her and Howie as husband and wife were a bad combination.

As I look at the staggering numbers, Sera arrives home from work.

"Still at it?"

"Yeah. The amount of money he stole is insane. I'm not sure if that bothers me more than the fact my father didn't see it."

She kisses me and asks, "What are you going to do?"

"I don't know. I could loaf around for a little bit, open my own firm, or work with you at Seaside."

"All three are solid options. Do you plan to share this with your father?"

"Hell yes! Howie needs to be held accountable."

"Let's eat dinner. Maybe you'll have an epiphany as to the best decision after some delicious pizza."

"Deal."

We eat, but there's no serendipitous moment for me. I'm pissed and don't really have anywhere to put the anger. I did nothing wrong. In fact, I did absolutely everything right. I put my nose down, made stupid sums of money for Calloway Investments, and could lose it all. Instead of simmering more, I decide to lighten my mood.

"What do you say to exchanging the rest of our gifts now?" I suggest.

"Sure, I guess. Do you want to stew some more?"

I shake my head. "It won't matter. At this point, my plan is to present the report to my father and hope he can find a way to do right by me. Otherwise, I may be unemployed soon because my brother was greedy."

"I'm sorry," she offers. Her hands cover mine, and she kisses me lightly.

"Me too."

Penny is a great model for Teddy and Maggie. I command her to stay while we retrieve our gifts. Sera decorated a tiny tree this year. Hiring Lex's decorator next season for our home wouldn't surprise me.

"Good girl. Good boy." I praise the pups and wait for Sera to return. When I adopted Penny, I didn't opt for the training program. For the new dogs, Lex and I decided it would be smart. It was worth the extra wait and cost to have a crate-trained puppy along with basic obedience already included.

Sera returns with two small gift bags and sits beside me on the couch in her formal living room. I suppose this would be called the drawing room since there's another space with a couch and television on the opposite side of the main floor.

"Open this one." She gives me the green bag.

I pull out the card and skim the words.

"Is this place local?" She rented an indoor soccer field for three, two-hour blocks for us, to see who is better or at least have fun playing a sport we both love.

"Yes."

"Just us or will your family be joining?" I ask.

"Up to you. A few of us are pretty good. What about Brax and Joe? Do they have any foot skills?"

"Worried I might know a ringer or two?" I probably do, but they are definitely not in the Mystic area.

"Perhaps."

I grin widely. "This is fantastic! When are you free?" Seraphina Soren, a billionaire heiress, gets me. Finding her has been the only bright spot of the year. Part of me wishes we met sooner, but I wasn't ready before now. Penny jumping on Sera was a stroke of luck. I'm grateful.

"We can schedule the date first thing next year," she replies.

"It's perfect. You better start training."

"Ha. Speak for yourself. Want the second one?"

I shake my head. "No, let's trade off." I hand her the envelope first.

She tears into it and pulls out tickets to the World Cup semifinal in Atlanta. "Wow! Crazy!" She extends the envelope beside her toward me. "Open this please."

I frown. I was expecting a different reaction. When I see tickets to the World Cup final, I burst out laughing. "Guess we're going to be traveling next summer."

"Yes, we are."

"When did you buy these? I tried but wasn't successful. I settled for the semis."

"I know a girl."

"Please explain."

She laughs, and my ears smile. I know that can't really happen. The sound of her happy soothes me to my core.

"My sister's college roommate, Lily, was besties with Leo, who is now her husband. Leo played pro football. His agent is my girl, Madeleine Wilton Anderson. She's the owner of Scala Talent and Sports Management. She can get into any event anywhere in the world."

"You used up that kind of goodwill for me?"

"Yes. Well, us. I'm joining you."

"Oh, I see."

Sera frowns. "You didn't expect me to bring you to the semifinal match? You don't want to come with me?"

"Expect? No. Wish, hope and pray. Yes. Want to spend every minute possible with you? Absolutely." I lean in for a kiss, and we make out on the couch until the dogs bother us. We let them out into the backyard. Thankfully, an area close to the house is fenced. Perhaps sometime in the past Anne had a pet or the previous owner had children. It's helpful because Sera would lose her mind if they destroyed the garden. I assume it is spectacular the rest of the year.

"Want to turn in?" she asks. "We have a big day tomorrow."

I shrug and return to the living room.

"What just happened? Your mood shifted, and—"

I cut off her words with her final gift hanging from my finger.

"I didn't realize there was more."

Extending the bag in her direction, she tosses the tissue paper playfully. I'm met with silence for a solid minute after she opens the bezel set solitaire necklace. The stone is about two carats. Large enough to stake my claim but not pretentious.

"Did I? No. I know I didn't. Did I?"

My stomach dips as if I overstepped somehow. I'm worried by her reaction to the gift. I draw her into my arms and whisper near her ear, "What, sweetheart?"

"Nothing. It's stunning. I love it. I always wanted one."

Her quick shift doesn't sit well with me. "You're welcome. Please share."

She draws her lips into a tight line and takes a deep breath. "My parents, well…, whatever. Ellery was gifted a similar necklace for her sixteenth birthday."

My heart sinks. She didn't get one, but her half sisters did. "I wasn't aware."

"In this moment, I realized my mother was lying my entire life. Cecile Soren knew her indiscretions would cost us. She just hid it well… for years. Then waited for the shoe to drop decades later. I get it, it seems backward. Wouldn't she give Baldwin's daughter diamonds? No, she would bestow them on her daughters who wouldn't end up heiresses."

"We can exchange it for earrings if you want."

"No. I meant what I said. It's beautiful. I love that it's from you."

I'm not sold on her statement. She's hurt and rightfully so. Sera won't lie to me. I take solace in that fact. "Let's get some sleep." Normally I prefer resolution and happy thoughts before bed. Tonight will be an exception to my loose rule.

With three puppies in tow, Sera and I arrive at my apartment near dinnertime on Christmas Eve. We left after she closed the store at noon. The traffic was horrendous. I had it cleaned last week so the staleness is minimal. Penny rushes in with Teddy and Maggie, who are hot on her heels exploring the space. We settled on those names after spirited debate. We put our luggage and leftovers on the island.

"Your home appears eerily similar to the cottage."

I nod my head. "It does except…." I stalk over to her and draw her into my embrace. "It's missing one thing."

Sera frowns.

"We haven't kissed here."

She winks and presses her lips to mine. I tug her lower lip between my teeth, and our tongues battle for supremacy. Our moment is short-lived. The dogs are weaving between us. They want to walk. I don't blame them. We've been stuck in the car for longer than necessary with the holiday rush. We put leashes on them and walk along the shore for a bit. Despite it being late in the year, the temperature is unusually warm with no snow on the ground and none forecasted in the near future.

It's in the low fifties, and we walk the entire length while discussing my plan for Howie.

"The last time we talked, you were still deciding what you wanted to do. Have you made a choice?" Sera asks while looking straight ahead.

She knows this is difficult for me.

"I don't want to lose Calloway, but unless my father is willing to change the trust before my brother's birthday, I'm screwed. The only way around the provision is either a sale of Calloway or an amendment. If the evidence and admission from Howie is enough, I'll keep running the business but from Mystic. If you'll have me."

"Yes, please," she replies. "If not?"

My lips pull into a straight, tight line. "Still working on that."

"I'm here to listen when you're ready."

"I know." I smile, and we finish our walk for this evening. We eat the leftovers from Sera's family meal and climb into bed.

First thing on Christmas morning, I sneak away and take the dogs out. My apartment isn't decorated, but I'm fine with it. We're meeting at my parents for brunch at eleven.

When I return, I make coffee and bring it into my bedroom. Unlike the last time Sera slept in my bed, her nakedness doesn't strike me as odd. Sera runs hot and prefers next to nothing for comfort almost daily. I love waking up with her. More importantly, I love that she isn't shy about her body.

When I push the door open with my foot, she stirs and sits up, baring her breasts to me. "Merry Christmas to me."

Sera rolls her eyes, scoots back, and tugs my shirt overhead.

"That's just mean and on a holiday!" I laugh heartily.

"I was hoping to start off with a light note for the day."

"I appreciate that. I'm not in charge of my professional destiny anymore. I hate it, but it's my reality."

We enjoy our coffee and get ready for brunch. My parents are a short drive away at least mileage-wise, but the commute will be at least thirty minutes to get there. They live in a townhouse on the Upper East Side of Manhattan. The property is perfect for them and includes an integral garage and private terrace. If I recall correctly, they moved here about five years ago after selling our family home in the suburbs.

My mother greets us when we arrive. "Sera, lovely to see you again. Ashton, thank you for coming."

"We appreciate you having us," Sera answers on our behalf.

Without question, she knows today is going to be difficult for me. Ruining our holiday meal isn't my intention, but it will likely be the outcome.

I prepare a cup of coffee for us, and we take a seat. Our discussions are light and about Seaside and other unimportant topics. While attempting to maintain an aura of calm, I'm reciting my words in my head. I hope my mother is none the wiser. I'm confident the same can't be said for my father. He's read the report himself.

"Are Howie and Nina joining us?" I ask my father, who joined us soon after our arrival.

My mother fidgets in her seat and replies tactfully, "They were supposed to arrive when you did."

"I'll call him," my father offers and excuses himself.

I'm lost in my head, but the ladies are discussing Sera's reading program with the puppies. Sera never fails to be aware of when I need support. While they chat, she sidles closer and takes my hand in hers. All my preparation could be for nothing if Howie doesn't bother to show. Is a confrontation necessary? In my opinion, yes. I need my brother to admit he stole from the company. It's likely my only chance to save it.

My father's expression tells me Howie isn't coming anytime soon, if at all. "Howie and Nina will be here early afternoon. We should eat."

The meal is enjoyable. The catered food ranges from French toast casserole to eggs Benedict to chicken Parmesan sliders. Our conversation stays away from politics and anything unnecessarily heavy. Much to my surprise, we talk extensively about soccer and the upcoming World Cup. I didn't realize my father was a fan. It isn't as if he ever watched me play. He never attended any of my games for any sport. I intend to remedy that with my own children should I be lucky enough to have some.

When the thought of children crosses my mind, my brother and niece breeze in through the front door. The arrogance of him choosing not to knock when he has never lived here grates on me. It's one thing to enter your childhood home without announcing your presence. Walking into anyone's residence without… ugh! Perhaps my disdain for my brother regarding the company increases my annoyance with him overall. I want to throttle him but the pleasure of leading him to his demise seems much more palatable.

"Hi, Mom. Dad. We're here," Howie announces loudly. Nina simply enters and greets her grandparents.

"Hi. I'm Nina." She waves to my polite, gracious woman.

"Sera."

She nods. "The girlfriend?"

Without missing a beat or taking the statement wrong, Sera says, "Yes."

I can only imagine that Nina saw the papers. My hope is Christine explained the flaws with Howie's behavior.

My brother doesn't bother to greet me. He states, "We're going to eat now."

Nothing bristles my mother, but today she speaks up. "No. Brunch was served earlier. You were two hours late. It's time for the gift exchange."

Howie frowns. "I didn't buy any."

"Very well. We'll sit in the drawing room, and my granddaughter will open her presents," my mother directs. "Nina, right this way. Your father, uncle, and grandfather have a few things to discuss."

That last statement is precisely why Sally Calloway is the personification of the perfect corporate wife. She may not be on the board or even work for the family company, but my mother is fully aware of the goings on. The fact it's a national holiday doesn't matter to her. Progress is necessary, and she's given me the chance to do it.

Sera and I follow my father into his office. We take a seat on the leather couch near the wall. Howie joins after assuring Nina he'll be there soon. Doubtful, but whatever.

"What is this about? I much prefer being with my daughter during my parenting time."

Ha! My brother is a crappy father and believes throwing money at Nina will do the trick. While I would like to approach this discussion meaningfully, it isn't going to happen with Howie's demeanor as it is today.

"How long did you think you were going to get away with stealing from the company?" I ask my brother pointedly.

"What are you talking about?" He rocks on his heels back and forth as if I touched a nerve. "If you're going to accuse me of malfeasance, she needs to go."

I grin at him. "Oh Howie. Despite your crude remarks and lack of information, Sera is well-educated and has degrees in business that you don't. She runs a long-standing, successful business. Her presence will help me remain as calm as possible during this discussion."

My father has been fully briefed on Norah Blackthorne's findings as well as the probability that Howie hid assets from Christine in their divorce. His reaction was private, if you will. Meaning my father didn't show his emotions to me at all. It isn't surprising to me. He has always been a stoic and even-keeled man. Sera extends the folder of evidence toward me. She has been a great help in hashing out how he pulled this off right under my father's nose.

Howie doesn't push his objection to Sera remaining in the room. I continue, "The first inkling something was up is the fact that both of my recent proposals were summarily rejected."

My brother scoffs at my statement. "Not my fault you don't understand the nuances of my type of business owners."

I shake my head. "That's laughable. I'm exceptional at reading people and figuring out the best arrangement for any company."

"Clearly not if you failed to find any new business because you were spending time with her." Howie points his crooked index finger at Sera.

I could come back with the truth that Sera was reluctant to date me at first but don't bother. It'll fall on deaf ears. My woman is ready to pounce on my brother, and I'm grateful. She could make him scream for mercy with words alone. She may not have thick skin like her brother, but her wit more than makes up for it. I glance at her and mouth. "I've got this, but I deeply appreciate your willingness to squash him."

Sera smiles and acknowledges my statement.

I press on, "At first, I chalked it up to not having the right approach for a wealthier small town than others I've worked in. The truth was so much simpler. You took my proposals from the company server, modified the margins to benefit one of your personal companies, and stole them from the family business."

"You can't prove any of that." He shifts and steps back. His words and his actions don't match.

I stand and laugh in my brother's face. "Not only can I prove it, but I can bury you in family court because you created the companies while you were still married to Christine."

That shuts him up for a moment.

My father, who until now has remained silent, asks, "How could you steal from this family?" As when I shared these findings initially, he remains calm and steadfast.

"I was taking what should be rightfully mine."

An admission, hopefully that is a plus for me. Not what I expected though. My brother never showed patience, compunction, business acumen, or desire to run Calloway Investments.

Mitchell Calloway rises to his feet and stands in front of his older son. "Why? You had more than enough money to live on from your salary. Nina is well taken care of."

Howie's eyes widen, and he charges toward me. I hop up and stand in front of Sera. My brother stops mid-charge. Why? I'm not certain. This time I will retaliate. There is no photographer, and my brother wouldn't dare press charges knowing I have evidence of him from before. "He doesn't deserve to run the company. He's younger and less experienced. My clients bring in more than his."

"Not true. Ashton's section of the company has been supporting yours for the last four years. The same timeframe you were working for yourself on the company's payroll." My father meets his false assumption with facts. Those details came from Norah's accounting without a doubt. Hiring Blackthorne may have been worth every single penny.

My brother becomes increasingly agitated as this conversation continues. He's pacing the length of our father's desk. He pauses every few steps, poised to respond but doesn't.

"What do you have to say for yourself?" my father asks.

"I can't go to jail. Christine will take Nina from me." My brother laments the predicament he's put himself in. I'm halfway between cheering and distraught on his behalf. "Is there a deal to be made?"

Spoken like a crook who got caught. I didn't dig deeply into the criminal or civil charges my brother could face. Off the top of my head, fraud, tortious interference with contracts, and maybe embezzlement would be on the list. The only good news is Calloway is a private company. We don't have to report him to the authorities, although we should. I don't foresee him learning his lesson.

"Honestly, prior to these facts coming to light, my inclination was to sell. An option that is still on the table. Your admission gives me pause. Ashton doesn't deserve to lose his livelihood because of your stupidity and greed. I'm going to take some time to consider all avenues."

"Thank you," I state.

"In the meantime, you will be cut off from all Calloway Investments servers and buildings. None of our research or systems will be available to you personally any longer. Until I determine the finer details as it pertains to the bylaws and trust, you will remain an employee. If you breathe a word of this conversation to anyone, I will without hesitation turn this forensic accounting over to the authorities and let them handle you."

Ideally, this last part gets him around the trust provision. The truth is the business that my brother stole was in his area of expertise. Swooping in and taking the two I worked on in the Mystic Cove area was petty. It also doesn't bode well for the future of me and my brother coexisting in the family company.

"How am I supposed to run my business without the computers and…." He clams up when he realizes the gravity of my father's statement.

"Not my problem. You stole clients, analysis, and revenue. Now, you need to figure out how to be a CEO on your own. My capital, business structure, reputation, and hard work are no longer available to you. Do you understand and acknowledge these terms?"

"Yes," Howie replies sheepishly.

I nearly correct my father but refrain. It's my hard work but his capital. I don't trust my brother as far as I can throw him, but I don't have a choice but to follow my father's lead.

"Happy now?" Howie sets his sight on me.

"With this meeting? Not at all. I would've preferred to maintain my position that you were simply below average as an employee. Instead, I have proof you're a thief, a liar, and a fraud. More importantly, those attributes likely contributed to destroying our family legacy."

Howie doesn't have a comeback for that. I'm confident he was expecting me to feel sorry for him. I don't. Not. One. Iota.

I reach back for Sera's hand. She stands, and we exit the office. This conversation isn't over. I shared my position regarding the company. Ideally, there's a way around the trust and bylaws. If not, I may need to come up with a deal of my own.

We join my mother and Nina. Sera presents her with our gift, a necklace with her initial and matching crystal bracelet. Despite having Howie for a father, she's gracious and thanks us.

We make our exit before Howie returns to the gathering. It's probably best right now to keep space between us.

"Want to talk about it?" Sera asks as we arrive at my apartment.

I shake my head. "Nothing more to add. I'm no longer in control of my career, and it sucks."

She encircles my waist with her arms and sets her head on my chest. "I'm sorry."

"Me too." I scan my apartment, and a modified plan materializes. "Do you think my clothes and personal items will fit in the back of your SUV?"

"Yeah. Why?"

"What do you say we go home… tonight."

A wide smile appears on her face. "Point me to what you want to pack."

I kiss her deeply, and we prepare to move me out of my apartment and into her house for good.

CHAPTER TWENTY-THREE

SERAPHINA

"Hi, honey. I'm home."

Ashton. A swell of joy and happiness comes over me. He's only been gone for the day, but it was a long one. I hurry from the kitchen to the foyer and throw my arms around him.

"I wasn't expecting you until later. How were the interviews?"

Instead of answering, he kisses me like it's been years not hours. Home, his lips on mine is safety and warmth and love. My hope is that we can emulate the partnerships around us like my grandfather has and Ashton's parents have.

"Better. What was your question?"

I laugh and lead him into the kitchen. The Carrara island is covered with papers. "How was your meeting?"

"Productive. I'll share more. What's all this?"

"Prospectus, annual reports, and an agenda for the board meeting."

"Nice. Can you order dinner while I change? Then we can chat about everything?"

"Sure. Italian or Thai?"

"Thai, please." With a light peck on the lips, he disappears.

Like me, Ashton prefers to be comfortable at home. He ditches the suit and tie and replaces it with shorts and a tee immediately upon arriving. I order our faves and continue reading.

I'm not surprised Celt is doing well despite losing our father. Sumner built the business from the ground up. My father took over about ten years ago. Grandfather stepped in for a short time after his death until Lex could get up to speed and deal with our mother. It's been slightly more than a year since my father's choices, both physically and personally, caught up with him.

The agenda for tomorrow's meeting sets forth adding me to the board, officially voting Lex in as the chairman, approving the transfer of my loft, and making an amendment to the bylaws regarding succession. Despite moving into the house, I want to keep my loft. More succinctly, I desire to own the building. I have some ideas for the expansion of Seaside, sort of but that is for later.

Ashton returns. While I set the table, the doorbell rings, and he retrieves our dinner.

We set out our curry dishes, pad Thai, and tom yum soup.

Ashton begins to share after a few hearty bites. "Do you know Cash Morgan?"

"I know of him. He's friends with Lex from his York Beach days. Plus, they went to boarding school together, I think. Continue anyway."

"Cash is from New York originally. He was an investment banker but leaned more toward pairing new businesses with angel investors. He also had a love of flying and piloted on the weekends. Then he bought an airline and left corporate investing altogether. That said, he suggested a few of his former coworkers as a good second for me."

"How confident are you that your father will follow through?"

Ashton purses his lips and ponders my question between bites. "As much as he hates the idea of cutting Howie off, I believe he has no choice. His independent forensic accounting found the same issues as Norah Blackthorne. He can't say I doctored the information to steal the company from my brother. To me, Howie made his choices. My father needs to accept that fact and make my brother live with them."

"How much time does he have left?"

"Two weeks. He needs to amend the trust and bylaws before Howie's thirty-fifth birthday on February 20th."

"If he sells, then what for you?"

He pauses as if he hasn't been thinking about this for at least the last two months. "I'm going to take a staycation. Then I will probably open my own firm. To be honest, I wouldn't need to work. If he liquidates the company, the trust corpus would be the proceeds. My father would have a fiduciary responsibility to make it grow to support future anticipated distributions for himself and me."

"Wouldn't you be bored?"

He grins at me and replies, "No. I would spend my days with you running Seaside and hosting 'Read to Puppies' to my heart's content."

"What would you have chosen as a profession if Calloway Investments didn't exist?"

"Never considered anything," he answers.

"Is that still what you want?"

Ashton ponders my question. "Honestly, I don't know. The only thing I'm confident about is our relationship. As far as my profession is concerned, if my father sells the company, I need to figure out what to do with my work life. The truth is there are numerous options. I love my job and don't want to find out I hate my other career choices."

"That sucks. I'm sorry."

"Me too."

We finish our meal. With a blanket for each of us, we let the dogs outside and curl up on the patio couch with the fire pit ablaze.

"Do you miss walking Penny?"

He laughs and shakes his head. "Not at all. I prefer relaxing with you."

"Good answer." I agree with him as well. We're a great match. I get butterflies when he arrives home. The money factor is nonexistent. In previous relationships, I was on edge with my initial trust. Weeding out gold diggers was a necessity. It's the reason my dating life has been sporadic. Most are adamant about dinner on the first date but not Ashton. He doesn't need or care about my wealth, current or potential. When he asked me out for coffee first, I knew he was different. My gut told me he was a keeper. I'm thankful his dog lost her manners nearly six months ago. More so, I'm ecstatic I was right about him.

First thing next morning, Ashton and I have coffee before my big day. I went into the depths of my closet to find an appropriate suit for the occasion. I opted for the navy one rather than the black I used for my father's funeral. Although I suppose wearing the same outfit would be ironic. He's gone, and I'm getting exactly what he didn't want. A woman who could run the company and have a seat at the table is against his plan for Celt. At least Sumner is forward-thinking.

"How are you feeling about the meeting?"

"Grateful. Vindicated and a tad angry that I had to wait for Lex for a Soren man to see my worth as far as the family business is concerned."

Ashton tilts his head. "That is unfair to Sumner, isn't it?"

I consider his question. "I suppose it is. The holdup was my mother. She thought Lex would capitulate. I'm thankful that part is done and Cecile Soren is no longer part of Celt."

"I never told you before, but it was hot as hell when you stood up for yourself."

"Thank you. It felt amazing to finally share my true emotions to her face."

Ashton kisses my forehead and adds, "Now you get to help Lex make decisions for your family business."

"He doesn't need me, but I appreciate the seat at the table nonetheless."

"Perhaps true."

"What is on your agenda for today?"

"I have a conference call with my father. Then, I'm not sure. I suppose my afternoon activities will depend on his decision."

I kiss him and turn to leave. Before exiting, I say, "He may surprise you." From a business perspective, I understand his father's predicament. It's more difficult for me on the family side because my own father didn't see me as an asset to the company like Ashton's does.

Ashton shrugs and wallows in his coffee a bit longer.

The drive to Celt is about twenty minutes. Upon arrival, Andrew greets me. "Morning, Miss Soren. Lex is in the small conference room. Mr. Sumner Soren has yet to arrive."

"Thank you." I walk down the hall with my head held high. From the moment I graduated with a business degree as required, I expected to be part of this company. Looking back, my father blocked me because he wasn't sure I was his flesh and blood. That cuts deeply. As does the reality he allowed Ellery to stay in her position despite the same reservations. I get it, she's a few years older and was ensconced in her role already. She kicks ass in the boardroom. Plus, she married Michael as he requested. I suppose that garnered her some goodwill.

Now, years later, the tables have turned. While Ellery still works for Celt, she doesn't have the same access and will never be promoted to the position she was born for. Well, the job she earned anyway. She was made for the CEO chair. Unfortunately, our mother ruined that for my half sister and her kids.

Lex is on the phone when I step into the modern conference room. My brother definitely upgraded the furnishings since I was here last.

"Yes, I understand." He ends the call and hugs me. "Hi, sis. How are you today?"

"Pretty good. You?"

He smiles. "That was Alannah on the phone. In concert with Attorney Alton, they believe they found a way to maneuver around the requirement that my child be a boy."

"That's good. Isn't it?" This would allow Lex and I to move forward sooner to close our father's estate.

"Yeah. It is. The provisions requiring marriage and a firstborn son aren't enforceable. Except—"

"There's still the issue about Waverly's inheritance or lack thereof," I state.

Before Lex can add more, Sumner arrives. "My apologies for my tardiness. I got a slow start this morning."

"No problem. It's only a few minutes," Lex states. "Let's begin."

I approach my grandfather and hug him. He appears to have lost weight since the holidays. "About time we're here for this."

"Thank you." I shoot Lex a text before taking my seat about my concerns regarding Sumner's health.

Lex stands at the head of the table and opens the meeting. "The first order of business on the agenda is to install Seraphina Soren as a full voting member of the Celt Industries Board of Directors. Please vote yea or nay."

Sumner covers my hand with his and says, "Yea."

Lex votes next. "Yea." The good news about a private company is that we can have as many or as few board members as we wish. For now, there will be three voting members. "Welcome, Sera."

"I appreciate you both immensely. I didn't see my father's behavior for what it was until… I had rose-colored glasses on. I won't let either of you down."

"We know," my grandfather replies. "I had been trying to remedy the situation for years."

I set my free hand over his. "It wasn't your fault. I have every confidence you tried to push my mother to do the right thing. It simply took longer than it should have. I appreciate your efforts on my behalf."

"You're most welcome," my grandfather replies.

Lex nods and continues with the agenda. In under an hour, I'm voted onto the board, the transfer of my loft is approved, and we amend the bylaws to allow succession regardless of gender.

Sumner grins at the conclusion of voting. "That was the most this board has accomplished in years."

"I agree," Lex adds.

My grandfather turns to me. "What do you plan to do with the building, Sera?"

"I want to open a Book Bar. The details are still a notion in my head. However, I want a comfortable, cozy space that allows people to drink the beverage of their choice and read with like-minded bibliophiles or bookworms."

"Your father was a fool for missing your talent for business," my grandfather replies.

"I appreciate that. My path may not have been what I wanted initially. In the end, I earned valuable experience and built my own livelihood." There was virtually no risk for me as far as survival. It would've destroyed me to ask my father for more money though. I suppose his failure to create a job through nepotism worked out in my favor professionally. Personally, I have a ways to go before I forgive him for choosing Lex merely because he was his son. His failure to request definitive proof of parentage sooner would've made his death easier to handle for us and our sisters.

"I suppose you did. I'll bid you farewell now. I have a standing chess game with Walter right after lunch."

"Careful, Wally is a shark in a penguin suit with an ascot," Lex warns.

Sumner, who has reached the door, turns back, "Who do you think taught him?"

We laugh and wave as our grandfather leaves the company headquarters.

My brother rounds the table and hugs me. "I'm crazy happy for you, Sera. When did you decide to use the boutique space?"

I frown. "I have some insider information from my boyfriend, sort of. His brother Howie offered them an infusion of capital to expand to a new location. If you haven't received the request to terminate their lease, you will soon."

"You want me to let them out penalty free," Lex asks.

I shake my head. "Absolutely not. Enforce the early release as much as the lease allows."

Lex cracks a sly smile. "Understood. Have you spoken with Lily yet?"

"Yes. I set up the accounts she recommended. I'm prepared for the transfer of my trust in a few weeks."

"Good. We have the same outlook on our wealth. You will have a sudden urge to purchase random things for a little while. Do it. I'm not suggesting you buy a super yacht, but a trip somewhere on your bucket list or a few pairs of red-soled shoes won't break the bank. I promise. Don't demonize your trust money like I did."

"Thanks. I appreciate the advice."

On a high, I wave to Andrew and exit the company headquarters. I'm giddy the entire ride home. After calling out for Ashton and checking his usual haunts, I start to worry. I pull off my shoes and search the entire house room by room. Then I realize the dogs aren't clamoring for attention. He must be in the yard.

Relief rushes through me when I see him playing catch with the dogs. I set down my heels and slide on the flip-flops we keep near the rear door.

"Hi. You okay?"

"I'm not sure."

My man needs time to process. I stand beside him and thread our fingers together. I have the urge to remind him I'm here, but I don't. The tension rolling off him is heavy. His demeanor leads me to surmise Mitchell decided to sell Calloway. To be honest, Ashton didn't share his true preference with me. He has been wrestling with his professional situation since before the holidays.

"The company will be split and Howie's half sold. My father intends to disown Howie."

Rather than give my opinion, I ask, "How do you feel about that?"

Ashton's shoulders drop in anguish. "He's going to hate me for a good while."

"Maybe, but you made the correct choice to preserve your family legacy."

Ashton adds, "I never wanted Howie to lose everything."

"He hasn't. Your brother has potentially lost immense wealth. Your family bond is more important than money."

He turns to face me and draws me close. "You're amazing. No woman has ever truly seen and understood me like you."

"Same here. I can be me, and it's enough."

"Always will be," he confirms.

"What does the sale mean for you?"

"I'm on my own. The proceeds will remain in the family trust. My half will be restructured, and I'll run it without oversight from my father."

"That's most of what you wanted, right?" I frown inwardly, as he doesn't seem thrilled.

"It is."

"Why aren't you happy about it?"

"Businesswise, I'm ecstatic. I did the right thing personally, but it stings. I had to destroy my brother."

"No, he did that to himself by defrauding the company. You brought his missteps to your boss. Integrity is always best."

Ashton sighs heavily. "You're right."

I wink at him. "Say that again."

He laughs. "Not a chance. How was your day?"

"It went well. We accomplished the entire agenda. I now own my loft building and want to share an expansion idea with you."

"Intriguing. Penny, Teddy, and Maggie, come." The dogs rush over and sit at our feet. "Good job."

For the rest of the afternoon, we discuss business and next steps for AD Calloway Investments and Seaside Book Bar.

"Talking shop with you is fantastic!"

I laugh, and we set goals and timelines for our businesses and trips for our soccer games this summer.

CHAPTER TWENTY-FOUR

ASHTON

Calloway Investments has been restructured in record time. Slightly less than a month later, I'm officially my own boss. I have full control over my schedule and the type of businesses we pursue. My focus will remain on similar retailers as before, but I intend to pursue exceptional deals if found from Howie's former wheelhouse. The escrow period allowed me to hire two staff members.

Stacy Sanders worked with Cash Morgan. If I'm not mistaken, Stacy assisted my friend with his airline purchase. He opted to remain in New York City and telecommute. He'll be traveling to the locations and reporting to me directly. He and his wife, Jocelyn, have two daughters.

My second hire was Adeline Hopkins. She's a recent graduate of Columbia with a dual degree in business administration and analytics. Addie's focus will be new business. She will work remotely as well. If necessary, I have access to some office space and the Morgan Family building.

Today's schedule is light because I'm preparing dinner for Sera in her garden for her birthday. The multi-seasonal space blooms in an organized manner. Sera enlisted Anne's gardener to assist her with care and upkeep. My woman isn't a fan of this day in general. A low-key celebration is in order. Her sisters intend to shower her with gifts and attention at Seaside. She should arrive home midafternoon. Matt and her newest hire, Quinn

Grady, have alleviated her need to be present all day, every day at the store. She can handle the books from here as she chooses.

I have a meeting with Lex myself in about ten minutes. It was at my request. The timing is coincidental. My nerves are off the charts. I cross the street and walk up the stone walkway and ring the doorbell.

Lex answers nearly immediately. "Morning." He looks exhausted.

"Hi. This can wait if you prefer."

He shakes his head. "Keeley didn't sleep well last night."

I acknowledge his words. "Neither did you."

"No. Would you like a drink?"

I wave him off and reply, "I'm fine, thanks."

We shift into the living room and sit facing their fireplace.

"How can I help you, Ashton?"

Need assistance not permission. "It's for Sera during our trip to London in a few months. I plan to propose while we're there, but I would prefer to maintain our privacy as long as possible."

"Congratulations! Sera will be pleased you didn't ask for my blessing."

I laugh. "She would."

"Whatever you need. I'll see what is available with your privacy concerns in mind."

"Thank you. I appreciate it."

"You and Sera are great together. I'm happy for you. If you need a lead on keeping your ring purchase discreet, please let me know."

"Will do." I rise and extend my hand to him. Instead, he hugs me. My chest feels tight. Is this what having a true brother is like? If so, I kind of love it.

"We're excited to have you join our family."

I smile. "The feeling is mutual."

"Lexington!" Keeley's voice echoes around me.

Sheer panic appears on his face for a split second. Then the future first-time father exudes calm. I'm surprised. My shock fades when I recall from a conversation with Sera that he was an EMT before returning home to run Celt.

He turns and meets his wife at the archway between the living room and foyer.

"What's wrong?" he asks.

Keeley grins from ear to ear and answers, "My water broke."

I approach them. "Why aren't you freaking out? She's not due for a few more months?"

Lex grins. "We fudged the timeline and details to keep my mother in the dark and out of Keeley's way. The last thing we wanted was our child's birth to be front page news for anyone other than us. She's only two weeks earlier than expected."

Perfect way to handle it. "Got it. How can I help?"

Keeley smirks. It fades quickly when she holds her abdomen and doubles over in pain.

"Her bag is by… Can you stay with her? I'll get the stuff." He disappears before he hears my answer.

"Of course." I shift closer to Keeley, and we step forward. "Do you need to change before you leave?"

Another contraction rises—her expression tightens and she exhales slowly. In addition, Keeley grips my arm harder than I've ever experienced before. When it passes, she answers, "I picked new clothes before I came down, but I didn't want to risk carrying the bags or cleaning the floor."

"Smart. Is there anything you need down here?"

Her brow furrows, and she replies, "My phone is on the island in the kitchen, and my purse is in the foyer."

"You good for now?" I ask and place her hand on the elegant molding.

She nods. As quickly as possible, I grab the items and return to her side. Outwardly, she seems calm for a first child. Me on the other hand, I'm freaking out, and it isn't even my baby about to join the world.

Lex returns, and I exhale slowly in relief. "Thank you, Ashton."

"You're welcome. I'll take Nala and Molly home with me."

"Thank you. I didn't think of that. Their leashes and stuff are in the mudroom."

"I'll find them. Congrats."

They exit hastily. I locate the dogs' supplies. With food, bowls, and blankets bagged. I thread my wrist through their leashes and walk home.

As I cross the street, Sera pulls into our driveway. She hops out and kisses me, then pets the dogs.

"Why are you walking Keeley's dogs?"

I inhale to answer, and my gorgeous, supportive woman starts jumping up and down.

"No way! Is she in labor? It's way early."

I wrinkle my nose. "About that… I asked the same thing, and your brother indicated they lied a bit to avoid drama with your mother."

Sera nods. "Makes complete sense. Yay! I might have a birthday twin."

"That's exciting to you?"

"Yeah, it is." Surprising considering her moderate dislike of her birthday. Her brow furrows, and she adds, "You made plans for tonight though."

I take her hands in mine and reply, "It's no problem. We'll work around a trip to the hospital. Although Keeley may prefer a visit at the house instead to afford them as much privacy as possible."

"Good point. It's what I would do."

I frown. "Make everyone wait until we're home before inviting guests to meet the baby?"

"Yes."

I agree. Plus, merging our families will have crazy headlines. Hell, a home birth might be the best choice. *Slow down, Ashton. Put a ring on it first.* I shake my head. "Sounds smart."

"How much time until my birthday date begins?" she asks with a slight lilt of excitement in her voice.

"The first part is set to go. Dinner isn't for a few hours."

Sera smiles widely. "Care to share?"

"Sure. Why don't you change your shoes while I let the dogs run outside for a bit?"

"Color me intrigued." Sera kisses me and skips away toward the main staircase.

"Come, guys. Outside." Five dogs hurry and sit near the French doors. They scurry down the steps and rush into the fenced area.

Fifteen minutes of furious running and chasing later, Teddy and Maggie are tuckered out near my feet. Soon, the others lope their way toward the steps and wait to be sent back inside. In succession, they plop onto the floor near the hearth and promptly fall asleep. Before I had Penny, I never understood the phrase "A tired dog is a happy dog." With five puppies snoring, it makes complete sense now.

Sera returns. I offer her my arm and guide her down the steps. My woman loves flowers, so I bought an insane amount of them and had a pathway constructed from the house to the garden. Each portion contains at least one for the flowers I gave her over the course of our relationship. If I'm the luckiest man on the planet, this is only the start of our journey with flowers.

Sera is quiet with awe. She slides her hand along my arm and threads her fingers with mine. The first arch includes roses, ranunculus, anemones, and alstroemeria in a pink and lavender. An exact replica of the flowers I gave her first. Then she progresses to buttercream roses. We're about halfway through the arrangement, and Sera asks.

"Are you trying to make me like my birthday again?" she asks as we continue along the path.

"Perhaps. Is it working?"

Sera purses her lips and whispers, "Maybe a little. Why are birthdays important to you?"

"It's the only day that is solely about one person. All other occasions are shared with someone else like an anniversary or graduation. Everyone, almost anyway, gets this celebration to themselves. It should be about that person and no one else."

Sera stops walking, turns, and kisses me deeply. "These are stunning. Thank you. I promise to try and embrace my birthday going forward with you."

"I promise to help you do it. Do you want your actual gift now or later?"

She opens her mouth to object but doesn't. "Later. Can we lay down and admire the flowers for a bit?"

"Absolutely." Proud that the flowers were well received, we lower to our backs and stare at the pops of color above us. I'm not sure exactly how long we lay there with our fingers threaded between us, but it's perfect.

The silence is broken by her phone vibrating in her pocket. She looks at the screen, and a wide grin appears on her face.

Sera reads the text aloud. "We're at the hospital. Keeley is doing great. I'll keep you posted when our little girl arrives."

"Family group text?"

"Yeah. I expect it to blow up a little given everyone thinks she is crazy early."

The instant the words left her lips, her phone starts buzzing incessantly. Rather than interrupt our time more, she silences her phone and retakes my hand in hers. "Ready?"

"For what?"

"We need to move under the next arch."

I laugh. "Sure." We wiggle along the runner the florist placed on the grass and stop beneath the buttercream roses. We repeat admiring and shifting down the path until we reach the end of the aisle and the red roses and eucalyptus.

"Want to have dinner now?" I ask.

At that moment, her stomach grumbles. Her soothing laugh surrounds us before she answers, "Yes."

Once I'm on my feet, I assist her to hers, and we walk inside. The pups are still chillin' near the hearth.

"I'll feed them."

I kiss her and continue on into the kitchen. Cooking isn't a specialty of mine, but there are a few dishes I can manage like an expert chef. I pull the salad from the fridge, give it a toss, and add the croutons. The bread will take a few minutes to brown.

As much as I would love to serve her, we each grab our plates and wine and walk back out to the garden.

"There's more?"

I shake my head. "The florist didn't really do anything in the garden. In fact, she was in awe and requested the name of our landscape architect."

Sera frowns briefly. "Did you let her down easy?"

"Yeah, I did." We eat in comfortable silence. I don't feel compelled to fill the dead air with unnecessary words. We can discuss any topic, but we don't need to speak incessantly. I love that about her.

"I think you should have dinner duty at least three times a week."

I grin at her. "Fine with me. What about the other days?"

Sera purses her lips and answers, "I'll handle two and we have takeout or a date night for the rest."

"I'm in. Was there an update when you were taking care of the dogs?"

Sera shakes her head. "No. I didn't expect one. Lots of well-wishes from my sisters though."

"I imagine it's hard for your sisters to have joy for Lex and Keeley."

"The whole situation is awful. The clauses for marriage and a son aren't enforceable. Elle, Sky, and Wave aren't going to contest the will. A fight was never what they were looking for. It's the exact reason Lex and I want to provide Wave with the same support as Elle and Sky."

"Your desire to treat her equally is admirable. Legally, it won't be easy though."

"I know. Since the lawyers shared the last update, they're working on how to give our youngest sibling a share of the estate."

"Now you wait… again."

"Yeah. I didn't feel any different when I woke up this morning despite the significant increase in my net worth overnight."

"That statement is precisely why your desire to provide for Waverly is genuine."

She smiles weakly and says, "Thanks. I don't want to cut my sisters out of my life, but I could understand any animosity they may have toward me and Lex."

"If anything, it should aimed at your mother."

"You have a solid point."

I wink at her. "I know. How about we talk about your birthday gift instead?"

Her eyes light up. My gorgeous woman can take this trip on her own and pay for it. The fact I can give it to her makes me giddy just the same.

I slide the envelope that was at the table in her direction.

She tilts her head in question.

"Were you expecting more jewelry?"

Sera shakes her head. "No. Curious is all."

"Open it."

Joy and awe pass over her face as she reads the destination and itinerary for our trip.

"Really? We're going to London in two months?"

A sparkle in her eye tells me her cake is going to have to wait.

"Absol—" My reply is cut off with her lips meeting mine.

"Race you to the bedroom."

I give her a quick peck on the lips and run toward the house. Her laugh trails behind her as she passes me effortlessly. We spend the rest of the evening tangling up our sheets.

Just before ten, we share a slice of cake in bed and turn in. Secretly, I think Sera was hoping for a birthday twin. The odds don't look great right now.

My goal was to have Sera enjoy her birthday again. I'm taking the win and looking forward to our first vacation together.

EPILOGUE

SERAPHINA

TWO MONTHS LATER

The weather is gloomy, but I don't care one bit. It isn't rainy or cold, so that's a plus. Ashton and I arrived in London two days ago. Despite my niece being only a few months old, Keeley and Lex are caring for our dogs. Her full name is Evangeline Cara Soren, and I love it. I was unlucky in my birthday twin quest, but I'm fine with a birthday neighbor instead.

"Ready, sweetheart?" Ashton asks from the balcony of our hotel. I accepted my brother's advice and went all out for this trip. Our accommodations are luxurious and overlook the Thames River. We've visited Westminster Abbey and Buckingham Palace already. The architecture is spectacular.

I nod and then ask, "Where are we going again?"

He crosses the room and kisses me deeply. "To the London Eye. Then we're cruising along the river for dinner."

"So two days from now is the trip to Warner Brothers?"

Ashton grins. "Yes, my love. We'll see the magic of Harry Potter before we go home."

My inner nerd is screaming. I love those books, and the opportunity to walk the sets and geek out is going to be phenomenal. With the reminder, I grab a sweater, and we greet our driver outside the lobby.

Instead of fussing with cabs or the tube, which is the subway in London, we opted to hire a car for our stay. It's quite convenient. Ashton insisted on it as well as using Pemberton Airlines. The perks of flying private are plenty, but my favorite was the passenger list included only us plus the crew.

We're whisked away to the base of the iconic Ferris wheel. Ashton and I are immediately escorted into a private pod complete with flowers and champagne.

He isn't. Oh my.... I reel in my thoughts and decide to live in the moment. To be fair, flowers aren't a rare occurrence with Ashton. The attendant closes the door, and we gaze out over the river at the sights. Big Ben and Parliament are visible on our right.

"This is amazing!" I admit and hug him close. His body is coiled tight with tension.

"Sera," he murmurs softly.

I shift and look at him. A closed velvet box is now in his trembling hand. He's nervous. Why? We're great together.

I move closer and whisper, "What's wrong?"

He takes a slow breath. "Nothing. For years, I've wanted to be here. Not in London but with the woman I love. We've only known each other for a short time, but... I don't care what societal norms say are correct. Only your opinion matters. I fully understand your reluctance to marry someone rich.

The same holds true for me. We balance each other out and can talk about nearly any topic. You and I can have the fairytale marriage we both desire. Together." He pauses.

Love and joy swell in my heart and mind. When Lex shared he knew from the moment he saw Keeley again, I'll admit I didn't understand. Until Ashton—well Penny—appeared at the right time. My soul understood he was the one for me. His slow approach was precisely what I needed to trust him and us for the future.

My gorgeous man continues from one knee before me. "Will you spend the rest of your life with me?"

"Yes. Yes!"

Ashton scrambles to his feet and sweeps me into his arms for a passionate kiss. We toast to us and make out some more.

When we come up for air, I ask quietly, "What's in the box?"

Ashton turns bright red. "I'm sorry. I was worried about conveying how much I love you…." He opens the small box, and my world stops spinning.

I never told anyone what my dream ring would look like and yet here it is.

Nestled in the cushion is a platinum ring with a channel set round stone. The band is softly curved and elegant. He plucks the ring out and slips it on my finger. I stare at the stunning custom piece for what feels like an hour.

"You hate it?"

I slide my hand to cup his jaw. "No. If I were to design my engagement ring, this would be it."

His shoulders drop in relief, and he kisses me again. We finish our champagne and gaze at each other and the sights until our ride comes to an end.

"I have one question. Did you ask Lex?"

Ashton laughs heartily. "He knows, but I did not request permission. I wanted his assistance to keep this as private as possible."

"That's why you insisted on the hired car and the private pod," I summarize.

"Among other things, yes. I love you, fiancée."

Suppressing the largest smile of my life is impossible. "I love you, fiancé."

We kiss and toast again before our dinner overlooking the Thames.

While we're celebrating our future nuptials, the situation goes downhill at home.

Thank you so much for reading *Unexpected Serendipity.*

Did you love *Unexpected Serendipity?*

Thank you for taking the time to read it. I hope you loved it!
If you liked this book or another one of my books, please consider
posting a review.
A short line or two will be perfect! It helps indie authors like me get
noticed. I appreciate your support and feedback.

COMING SOON

A Scala Talent & Sports Management Novel

MY BOOKS

Protecting Us

Hers to Protect

Protecting our Family

Protecting Home

Agent Protection

MATCHMAKERS' BOOK CLUB

For Love & Coffee

For Love & Basketball

For Love & Cookies

For Love & Photos

For Love & Invisible String

SCALA TALENT & SPORTS MANAGEMENT

Moonshot

Our Messy Sequel

THE SOREN FAMILY

Unexpected Forever

All my books in one place: www.nicolevidal.com/books